PRAISE FOR KENYA MOSS-DYME

"Kenya Moss-Dyme takes the Creepy Kid genre and weaves it through generational and genealogical trauma in a tightly bound descension of madness. *Progeny* is not for the weak."

— MO MOSHATY (*LOVE THE SINNER*)

"Children really shouldn't play with dead things, but they do in *Progeny*, Kenya Moss-Dyme's creepy tale of an adoption-from-hell that reads like *The Omen* meets *The Good Son*. Readers will find themselves rooting for asthmatic teen protagonist Craven amidst all the gory body transmogrifications and relentless bloodshed. Like the best horror, there is heart and heartbreak at the center of all the bloodletting, making *Progeny* a genuine standout. Lean and mean from its first page to its last."

— VINCE A. LIAGUNO, BRAM STOKER AWARD ® - WINNING EDITOR OF (*UNSPEAKABLE HORROR: FROM THE SHADOWS OF THE CLOSET*)

PROGENY

KENYA MOSS-DYME

Progeny includes content that might not be suitable for some readers. We've included a list of these elements at the end of the book. If you have concerns, please check it out so you can decide whether to continue reading.

CONTENTS

"They come through you but not from you, And though they are with you yet they belong not to you."
  Khalil Gibran

"Even a man who is pure in heart and says his prayers by night, may become a wolf when the wolfbane blooms and the autumn moon is bright."
  The Wolf Man, 1941

DEDICATION

Progeny is dedicated to Ebony Evans of the EyeCU Reading Club for inspiration during Freestyle Friday (2018). Originally conceived as Sibling Rivalry, it has taken on an entire life of its own but the seed was planted that day.

So happy to release it to the world.

PROLOGUE

Wind isn't supposed to howl like this.

It screamed through the trees, whipping the limbs back and forth so hard that they broke loose from the tree trunks and flew through the air. Branches tumbled on cars, breaking windshields, scratching paint.

It wasn't just a stormy night, it was a stunningly dangerous night.

Evangeline paced back and forth inside the small dimly lit wood-framed home where she had been summoned hours earlier. Contractions ripped through her body and she pressed her hands against her swollen belly, whispering angrily, "No! Not yet!"

As the pain eased, she knelt by the window and peered through the blinds, looking for sign of her absent host. The door was unlocked when she arrived and the house empty, but there were indications that he had prepared for her arrival. As Evangeline nervously explored the tidy home, she made her way to the bedroom where she found items prepared for the birth. Towels, blankets, a bassinet, along with a metal tray holding a stethoscope, thermometer and some other odd-looking medical devices she didn't recognize immediately. Standing in the doorway, she took in the scene with a heavy heart, emphasized by thunder and lightning that seemed to grow more intense with each passing minute.

Another contraction hit, this time even stronger than the last, causing Evangeline to cry out in agony. The sharp tips of her canine teeth cut into the tender skin of her tongue; blood spilled from the corner of her mouth and down the front of her dress. Catching a glimpse of herself in the dresser mirror across the room, she winced at the sight. Bloody, wet and wild, her canines automatically protruded in instances of fear, anger or stress.

This night checked all three boxes.

Her water had burst before she began the journey over so she knew that the time was near. But now, the jolts of pain were like daggers in her spine, sending her to her knees, helpless and afraid. She tried to hold onto the door frame and pull herself back to her feet, but her sweaty palms prevented her from taking grip and she collapsed, crying.

Outside in the storm, a black sedan with headlights off turned into the driveway of the house and sat with the motor running. A thunderous clap roiled out of sky and shot a bolt of lightning into the tree sitting at the edge of the front yard. The trunk split and a branch peeled away, landing just a few feet away from the hood of the sedan.

Moments later, a tall black man emerged from the driver's side of the car and stood next to the door; slowly turning his head left to right, he surveyed the storm-ravaged street as the wind angrily lifted the flaps of his coat and whipped them around his long legs. When he began walking toward the house, he raised one hand to secure his cap against his head, as the wind threatened to snatch it away by the brim and toss it down the street with the leaves.

Inside the house, the contractions grew closer together and a panicked and shaky Evangeline realized that she could no longer hold off her child's entrance into the world. Tearfully, she lowered her body to the floor next to the bed, using her elbows to support her weight as she got into an upright seated position.

"You can do this." A man's voice came from the darkest corner of the room.

Frightened, she twisted her head around to look for the speaker, to look for *him*, but there was no one there. Her eyes darted around in fear and she cried out, "Where are you?!"

"I'm here," the voice calmly replied. *"I am with you."*

The contractions subsided and her pelvis felt full as the baby began to slip into the birth canal.

Evangeline found the voice in her head to be soothing, even empowering. She ripped at her underclothing to prepare for delivery and she felt a sense of comfort as she braced her back against the bed frame and took a deep breath.

He was indeed there, *somewhere*. In her head, as he'd always been, watching her, protecting her when she needed it the most. As she focused on her lower body and bore down with all of her might, a primal-like scream erupted from her throat and the storm outside seemed to respond; the wind screamed back and the rain pounded even harder against the roof.

"Yes! Yes! You are doing it!"

A flash of lightning illuminated the room and the infant slipped free from her womb after the third push. A baby boy, whose entrance was welcomed by a deafening crack of thunder followed by a serenade of lightning bolts attacking the trees surrounding the house.

Feeling dizzy and weak, Evangeline's hands shook as she pulled one of the towels from the stack and gently wrapped the baby inside for warmth. Holding one hand up to her face, she stretched the fingers, stiffening them to allow the claws to extend from the tips. Fully extended, she used that hand and those claws to slice at the umbilical cord and disconnect herself from the infant so she could wrap him more securely in the towel.

"There, there," she cooed, rocking him gently. Suddenly, she froze as terrible realization began to settle.

"He should be crying! WHY ISN'T HE CRYING?" She screamed as she realized the baby's skin was a sickly pale shade of gray. His eyes were closed, she stroked his face, his neck, across his body, turning him over to compress his back in case his airway needed to be cleaned.

"WHY ISN'T HE CRYING?!" She screamed again, fighting against the dark waves beckoning her to close her eyes and sleep.

"I got him."

A dark figure stepped into the room and reached down, taking the baby from her arms.

"You can sleep now. Your job is done. You did good."

Evangeline struggled against the black but it was a war she knew she could not win. It had been chasing her for years and this time there was nowhere to run. She felt weak and her body slid down to lie on the floor.

The storm continued to scream and rage and seemingly shoot lightning directly at the house as Evangeline rested her head on the cold wood floor. She was listening for the sound of her baby's cry as she closed her eyes for the last time.

The mysterious man quickly exited the house carrying a bundle of towels between his arms. Rushing to the car, he backed out of the driveway and sped away before a single bolt of lightning struck at the roof and sent flames into the air.

CHAPTER ONE

CRAVEN DID IT

For the first time in his 14 years of living, Craven wished his parents were home.

As he raced and dodged furniture in the elaborately decorated living room, his rubber soles squeaked across the wood floors. He longed to hear his mother call from another room, "Craven, I just know you're not running in the house and scuffing up my floor!"

He cleared the living room and slammed into the wall with his hands raised, leaving a visible dent upon impact. His eyes watered, and Craven winced at the pain that shot from his wrists into his shoulders. No time to nurse his wounds, he had to keep moving. The door to the backyard was only a few feet away, and if he could just touch the doorknob with the tips of his fingers, then he'd be free.

His shoes were too noisy, they needed to go. Craven reached down and slipped them off his feet, bending forward to gently place them on the floor. Then he decided instead to hold a shoe in each hand, wielding them as weapons as he moved toward the door. The room darkening curtains hanging on the window seemed like a good place to hide, and he crept silently over and stepped into the opening of the heavy fabric.

"Where are ya, big brotha?" Craven heard his brother, Leo, whisper menacingly, the words drooling from his lips.

Craven watched his younger brother between two folds of curtain, fighting with every tendon in his body to stay still.

Don't breathe, don't even tremble.

"We can smell you," Leo hissed, turning toward the open doorway. He sniffed the air; Craven's bladder gave in and warm urine traveled down the legs of his jeans, eventually reaching the wood floor and spreading around his feet.. A whimper escaped Craven's throat as the curtain was ripped violently from its rod, exposing him to a face that he didn't recognize. Leo's lips peeled apart in a hideous grin that was far too menacing to be human. By instinct, Craven attacked with the shoes in his hand, swinging wildly and without strategy in a vain attempt to move Leo away so that he could continue towards the back door, towards freedom.

But his blows were no match for his brother, not *this* version of his brother, or that monstrous *thing* that stood guard behind him with its fat tongue hanging out of the side of its snout, panting, and waiting its turn.

CRAVEN EXPECTED some kind of blowback from his actions earlier, but he didn't quite prepare himself for *this*.

Seated on the couch, watching some football, Craven had his ear slightly tuned to the sound of Leo arriving home. He was waiting for a sign that his brother had discovered what he'd done. A yell, a cry of some sort, and

Craven would brace himself for the impending fight. But the sign came in the form of an immediate attack.

A breeze floated through his hair and he looked up just in time to brace for the weight of something large and hairy landing on his shoulders. Panic set in as his face was smothered in the grip of some kind of animal. Breathing filled Craven's lungs with a foul scent not unlike rotten meat buried within moist layers of fur.

He opened his mouth and screamed into the mass threatening to suffocate him, and used every last bit of his strength to slide down and to begin to crawl away. Suddenly, he heard the sound of footsteps running toward him, and then Leo was on his back, clawing at his face from behind.

When did this kid get so heavy?

Craven rose from the floor and sprinted across the room without looking back. He didn't know what Leo had become, or why he had turned into...whatever he was, but as he ran through the house with fear pounding in his chest, he just wished their mother was still alive to save him.

LEO

This had to be a joke.

Staring at his parents across the breakfast table, Craven first looked helplessly in his father's direction, then locked eyes with his mother, Claire. He held his breath, waiting - hoping - for the big laugh, the punchline. Craven felt his chest tightening. His father jumped up from his chair and began moving around the kitchen, pretending to be busy by scraping leftovers into the garbage can. His plan was to attempt an escape out the back door under the guise of taking out the trash, but Craven, being familiar with his dad's moves, stood up and positioned himself in front of the door.

"Wait...say what again, mom?"

"I said, we're bringing Leo home tomorrow," Claire repeated, louder this time. "You know, your little brother."

Craven scowled. "He's not my brother."

"You promised you would try, Craven. We've talked about this; you've had plenty of time to adjust."

"But you said the paperwork and everything probably wouldn't be finished for months!"

"It's been eight months. It's time for him to move in and become part of our family. He's just as ready as we are."

Paul, Craven's dad, let go of the trash can and shuffled over behind his wife's chair.

"This is great, right buddy? We finally got another player for driveway basketball!" He threw up his hands in a mock cheer. "Gooooo, Bennett boys!"

Craven pulled his inhaler from his jean pocket, removed the cap and shook it while scowling at his parents. He pressed it to his mouth and took a puff, breathing in sharply. "This shit sucks," he spat at them before turning to leave the kitchen.

Startled, Paul took a step forward as Craven left the room, slamming the door in his wake. "Hey! Watch your mouth, man!" Paul yelled at the door.

"Let him go, he'll be back when he calms down. He just needs to process it all." Claire sighed heavily and leaned back in her chair. 'It's a lot for him. Maybe it really is too soon."

"We did everything the way Pharaoh suggested. Spent all of these months letting everyone get to know each other, so I don't understand why..."

Claire rested her chin on her hands for a moment before slapping the tabletop and standing. "You know what? It doesn't matter. We're doing this. Craven can just stop being such a selfish spoiled brat."

"I don't know. I'm starting to think we shouldn't, maybe—"

"Having another kid in the house will be good for him," said Claire, then added. "That poor kid has been through enough. I'll be damned if we let him down too."

Paul groaned and shook his head. "I'm just worried that we haven't been totally honest with him about Leo's ... history."

"But if we tell him everything, he won't even give Leo a chance! We gotta let them just get to know each other and grow to love being brothers. Then we'll sit Craven down and tell him the rest. There's nothing he needs to know right now."

"Funny. I'm supposed to be the therapist in this marriage!" Paul laughed and covered Claire's hands with his own.

"It'll be fine. I promise," Claire continued with a smile. "Just wait until they meet. Who couldn't help but fall in love with the little kid? We did, and Craven will too!"

"But, will Leo fall in love with us? I guess that's the true test!"

They embraced and quietly held on to each other. A basketball struck violently against the side of the house and jolted them back to the reality of the day ahead, and the weight of the secret they were keeping.

THE CHILDREN LIVING at Humbolt Center had come from all over, with various backgrounds, experiences, and traumas. From toddlers to teens, they shuffled in and out of the white, wood-framed colonial, each one calling it home at different times and terms of their young lives. It was a place of peace for most; sometimes the first and only peace they'd known. For others, it was just one more layover in their itinerary of rejections.

Leo Foreman perched on the front steps of the home, just a few feet away from the road. The rush of wind from the speeding cars whipped around his face and lifted his curls in the air.

A brown, bushy-tailed squirrel darted back and forth near the edge of the street, trying to find a safe opening to slip to the other side. Leo chuckled as he watched the squirrel bounce against the spinning wheels of a sedan and jump back, rolling backwards across the grass. It paused and tried again, its fluffy tail swaying back and forth like a banner of determination.

Leo watched intently as the squirrel dove for a small opening between two cars before flipping back to the curb. His eyes followed the squirrel's every leap and bound, heart racing in tandem with the tiny creature's challenge to get to the other side of the relentless torrent of cars. Leo's palms grew sweaty as the squirrel made an especially daring dash across the asphalt and had its life tragically cut short with a sickening pop.

Leo hoisted his backpack and stood, then walked to where the squirrel lay, its tail flickering in a last hurrah. He scooped its shattered body into his hands, cupping it safely to his chest as the squirrel's warm insides dripped between his fingers. Its tiny heart beat slowed to a ragged stop, with a final shudder vibrating through the tiny body. The squirrel's skull was crushed, its eyes were closed, and its tiny tongue hung out the side of its flattened head. Leo raised the critter to his mouth, took a deep breath, and exhaled directly onto what used to be the squirrel's face. The tail fluttered weakly and brushed against Leo's hand.

This would be a nice addition to his collection. He'd never had a squirrel before.

Leo unzipped his backpack and dropped the lifeless squirrel inside where it landed atop the carcasses of its furry buddies.

He returned to his spot on the steps and sat, lightly patting the backpack to comfort the animals inside. Their energy vibrated softly through the rough fabric and he found that soothing.

"LEOOOOOOO!"

Ms. Pulaski barreled through the house, yelling at the top of her lungs. "Where is that boy? Natalie, have you seen Leo?" She stopped at the bedroom and questioned a young girl that was stretched across her bed and wearing head-phones. Annoyed at the interruption, the girl waved her off and continued nodding her head to the music. Sensing she would get no assistance here, the woman rolled her eyes and continued moving down the hallway, loudly yelling Leo's name.

He was usually tucked away in a closet or curled up in a far corner of the basement, admiring and counting his weird little animal corpses like marbles. She opened the basement door and stood still with her head cocked to the side, listening. Deep inside she was relieved that it was silent.

The last time Ms. Pulaski had to descend the stairs to get Leo, she'd encountered a terrifying scene that still haunted her to this day.

It was about a month after Leo had moved into the house, so he was still adjusting to the new environment and the other kids. Ms. Pulaski was giving him some grace to get to a point where he felt safe and comfortable, so she didn't bother him much when he would separate from group time to go hang out alone. But the house still had rules, and those rules were drilled into the kids when they arrived. There were no maids or cleaning services; everyone had to do their part in tidying up and maintaining the premises, even Leo. He'd pulled his first disappearing act after dinner when she was distracted with doling out tasks to help get the kitchen back in order.

When the night rolled in and Leo had not reappeared, she had decided to begin searching the most popular hiding spots in the house. In a cheerful mood, she had pulled back accordion closet doors while shouting, *"BOO!"*, but found nothing. She got down on her aching knees to look and poke around beneath beds and came up empty-handed. She had even enlisted the other kids to help by suggesting a treat as a reward for finding Leo. All to no avail.

Before she would resort to calling the police, she had decided to thoroughly sweep the cluttered basement one last time. Because the space was dimly lit with barely enough room to walk without tripping over boxes or furniture, the children knew not to play down there. But something told her that might be exactly the kind of place where Leo would love to play.

Although her skin crawled at the thought of the kinds of insects that could be lurking, she took a deep breath and hit the light switch, then made her way down the stairs.

When she reached the landing, she stopped and called his name.

"Leo? If you're down here, you need to speak up! I won't be upset if you come out from hiding right now!"

She heard a faint rustling sound a few feet to her right, in an area that the light didn't entirely reach. Her heart had raced as she slowly turned and felt her way around the stacked boxes, and a chill creeped up her spine just as an odd smell hit her in the face like a brick wall.

Feeling sick to her stomach, she paused and balanced herself against a concrete pillar. The odor was a mixture of something both rotted and damp to the point of mildew. Ms. Pulaski shuddered and whispered, "Leo, is that you?" She hoped he wouldn't answer and that she could turn and leave because the eerie stillness made it seem like even the walls were holding their breath, waiting for something to happen.

The rustling cut through the silence again and Ms. Pulaski had pushed herself away from the pillar to continue moving in the direction of the noise.

"Do that again," sounded a child-like voice just ahead of her behind the boxes, followed by a low, guttural growl.

Ms. Pulaski navigated around two more ceiling-high stacks of household items; then one final turn at the corner of the stack where her breath caught in her throat at the source of the sounds.

Leo had been sitting on the floor in a clearing, slightly illuminated from the bit of light that stretched across the ceiling from the stairs. His backpack was on the ground next to his legs, and he was hunched over what looked to be a pile of small, dead animals. His face twisted in deep concentration as he spoke gently to them.

His hands moved back and forth across their crumpled bodies and she was almost certain that she saw the pile shake and tremble as his fingers passed.

She felt sick to her stomach. She knew he was different than the others, but this was far beyond what she imagined different could be. Struggling to remain calm while searching for the right words, Ms. Pulaski had been acutely aware that she might even be in danger as they were in this secluded space of the basement. Footsteps crossed the floor upstairs as the other children went on with their evening without a thought about where she had disappeared to. It might have been hours before they even noticed she was gone. She knew at that moment that she needed to get out of the basement, even if it meant leaving Leo down there to his own devices.

A whimper had escaped her lips and caught Leo's attention.

"Hey, Ms. Pulaski. Were you looking for me?" His eyes shone with an eerie intensity.

"You...you shouldn't be down here alone, Leo," she whispered, hoping that he wouldn't notice that her voice was shaking with fear.

"Why not? I'm just playing with my friends." Leo replied softly, gesturing toward the tiny lifeless bodies scattered on the ground around him.

"Oops, I think I lost one."

"One...what? One what?" She asked.

He had dug his hands deep into the pile and spread the bodies apart, then he had begun poking them in their bellies as he counted. Their eyes – the ones that still had eyes – bulged out each time he pushed his fingers into their core, and their tiny mouths popped open.

That was all that Ms. Pulaski had needed to see before she spun on her heel and ran back in the direction toward the stairs. She scrambled up the stairs bent forward, using her hands to propel herself faster. She went straight to her cellphone and called the corporate office and let them know that they were certainly not paying her a high enough salary to deal with that amount of *strange*.

It took a few weeks of paid leave and therapy before the Leo's case manager convinced her that it was all a big misunderstanding. Surely her nerves, fear, and high blood pressure caused her to imagine that the dead animals were moving. He further explained Leo's unfortunate emotional attachment to his *pets* and assured her that he wouldn't be a resident for long, as he was already processing a kind couple to adopt the boy.

LEO NEVER HID in the basement again, but he still occasionally wandered off with his backpack.

Ms. Pulaski trudged through the house calling his name. Passing the window facing the front porch, she caught sight of the top of Leo's head from his seat on the stairs.

She burst through the door and onto the porch, panting heavily. "Leo! I know you heard me calling you!"

Leo ignored her and continued staring out at the traffic.

"Well, this is unbelievably rude! I've had enough of you. Off to bed you go!"

Leo sat frozen.

Angry now, Ms. Pulaski stomped down the stairs to the ground, positioning herself in front of Leo with her hands on her hips.

"I won't be ignored, Leo," she said through pursed lips and locked his eyes.

The road rumbled at Ms. Pulaski's back, vibrating through the sidewalk beneath her feet. She felt each passing car as it sped past, sending gusts of wind that tugged at her hair and clothes. But she also felt something frozen cold running in her veins, leaving her arms stiff and locked in position.

She tried to move her hands to drop her arms; tried to shake them to get rid of the tingling feeling that was now traveling through the length of her arms and into her fingertips.

Is this what a heart attack felt like?

Leo's eyes never moved from her face. He didn't blink,

didn't look away, he just *stared* as if he wasn't seeing her, but instead, was looking through her.

Ms. Pulaski began to panic and struggled to open her mouth to beg Leo to run and get help. But while she was unable to move her upper body, her feet sprang to life with a mission of their own. She felt her legs lift, one by one, and take backward steps, one foot behind the other.

Frightened, frozen, and unable to move her face to scream for help, her legs ushered her backward in a stiff, awkward gait that looked as if she were in a horror movie.

She glided quickly over the grass that divided the sidewalk from the asphalt, and stepped off the curb.

Car horns blared and brakes squealed as they were applied, but the traffic was going much too fast to come to an immediate stop. The impact from the first vehicle tossed Ms. Pulaski into the air. When she came down on the hood of another car, the traffic bounced her body like a bloody shuttlecock.

When it was all over, there was very little of Ms. Pulaski that was suitable for a final viewing.

Witnesses would later describe the horror that day as a woman willingly and deliberately, stepped backwards into speeding cars while a little boy sat on the steps just watching.

Not helping, but just...watching.

DEAD ANIMALS

Craven woke up early the next morning to start moving things around and out of his room. His goal was to hide all of his cherished items, or at least to put them out of the reach of the little vagrant that would soon be moving in. He had retrieved his old trunk with the built-in combination lock from the basement; now he stood surveying his room for any item that might be enticing to a kid – especially one coming from a less than privileged background. Craven quickly scooped his most precious possessions and dropped them into the trunk, from sports trophies to hand-painted rocks from summer camp, it all went into the trunk for safekeeping. Soon, the room was stripped nearly bare of anything that suggested that it was occupied by a teenaged boy.

"Not going to make himself at home in my room!" Craven muttered to himself as he hauled the heavy loaded trunk back to the basement. He stumbled on the stairs and the weight of the trunk pushed against his leg, sending him sliding down to the basement floor with the trunk at his back. Pain shot through his ankle as he hit the landing at an awkward angle.

Icing, meet cake.

Craven pounded his fists on the stairs, unable to stop the tears.

"It's not fair!"

He hadn't asked for a little brother. He hadn't asked for any of this. Especially not this weirdo kid that barely wanted to interact with him, much less join the family.

Leo wasn't exactly the poster kid for foster programs. He was quite the opposite of everything a parent dreamed of, and for Craven, he seemed like a nightmare loading.

There was a time in the past when Craven found the idea of having a little brother appealing. He'd hoped they might have one the "normal" way, but his mom had made it clear that wasn't on the table. By the time Craven's parents presented him with their plan, they had already started the initial adoption process and spent time with Leo at the foster home. Their minds were made up and that was that.

They gathered with Leo at the foster home in a bright little room at the back of the house designated as the Meet Up Station. It was a wildly decorated amusement park-themed playroom that provided a relaxed atmosphere to connect with the little human that you would be bringing into your home. There were plenty of distractions in case the conversation stalled or went sideways: a small carousel, life sized stuffed animals, a selection of motorized ride-arounds and carnival games, and an abundance of snacks within reach.

Paul and Claire had sat on the sofa, deep in discussion with Leo's case manager, a tall, imposing black man who scribbled furiously into a notepad as if he were dictating their conversation.

Craven had spent most of the time at the snack table against the back wall, stuffing both his face and his pockets with things he could eat on the long ride back home. At 8 years old, Leo couldn't hold the attention of a 14-year-old, but Craven was attempting to feel him out to see what kind of kid he really was, outside of his parents gushing over him, and outside of the information sheet they had been given days before the meeting. Craven was playing it cool, figuring that the best way to get to know Leo was to not act like he was trying to get to know him. He wandered around the room with a milkshake in one hand, sampling the games and toys while expressing how cool everything was.

Craven had felt the child at his back as he stood, reading the labels of the DVD movie selection. A breeze had gone through his jacket and he felt a presence closing in on him, and he turned to find Leo standing directly behind him. So close, in fact, that Craven would have crushed his small foot if he'd taken a step backward.

"Oh! Hey! What's up?" Craven had taken a couple of light bounces to the side as he turned to look at Leo. "How's it going?"

Leo had tilted his head and stared at Craven wordlessly. He had worn a baseball cap emblazoned with the logo of a sports team that Craven was not familiar with, and his eyes carried a dull sparkle beneath the brim of the hat. Tendrils of dark brown hair escaped from beneath the cap, framing a caramel-colored face with its rounded nose and deep eyes. The angelic visage was captivating at first, but just as quickly, the light in Leo's eyes evaporated and his expression was left blank.

"Who's that there?" Craven nervously took note of the

shift, but forged ahead with the ice breaker. He raised his hand to point at the hat and Leo jumped. "Hey, it's okay! Just checking out the hat, dude!"

What a weirdo. Geez.

Leo reached up and removed the cap, holding it in front of his face as if he'd never seen it before.

"I don't know. I got it out of the bin," he answered after a moment or two passed, then replaced the cap on his head.

"Looks cool. The logo looks like –"

"Wanna see my room?" Leo interrupted.

Before Craven could answer, Leo turned and began walking toward the doorway. Craven caught his mother's eye from across the room and shrugged with a look that asked for permission, but also thought this all very strange. In the back of his mind, Craven had hoped his mother would squash the idea of them leaving the relative safety of the open meeting room, but she simply smiled in his direction and turned her attention back to the counselor.

Seeing no way to avoid it, Craven sighed, then rushed to catch up with the kid. But by the time he got to the meeting room's door, he barely caught sight of Leo turning the corner at the end of the long and empty hallway. Craven moved quickly and managed to spot Leo standing outside the doorway to one of the rooms.

"You move pretty fast for a little guy," Craven joked as he hustled up beside him. He turned to squeeze past Leo and enter the open door, when Leo threw up his arm and blocked Craven by grabbing the doorframe. His sharp elbow hit Craven in his midsection. After a pause and with a grand swing of his arm, he waved Craven inside like a game show host welcoming the next contestant to the stage. He had a big toothy smile plastered on his face and it was disarming to Craven who was beginning to think Leo couldn't smile at all.

Once inside the room, the putrid smell smacked Craven dead center in his face. The odor draped itself around his head and shoulders like a weighted blanket and he couldn't inhale without the fear that the insides of his stomach would rush up to his throat.

Through watery eyes, Craven saw Leo dash past his side and reach for a backpack beneath the bed. Craven stumbled backward, reaching for the wall to steady himself, as Leo happily chattered, unzipped the backpack, and dumped the contents onto his neatly made bed.

"I bet you never seen so many pets, right? I mean, unless you go to a pet store! This is kinda like a pet store, right? I mean, it's a little different, I know, but still, it's pretty cool, huh?"

Craven had wiped at his eyes with the bottom of his tee shirt and tried to focus on the words Leo was speaking, but he felt a fire building in his chest as his lungs began to constrict. His brain screamed, telling him to run out of the room, NOW, but his feet would not move. He stood there with his mouth open as Leo stroked, pointed to, and described the menagerie of road kill spread across the blanket.

"I got a rabbit! And I named him Pecan Pie because he's like white but mostly brown because of these spots all over 'im,"

The rabbit's body was stiff and dried out, but as Leo tenderly ran his fingers across the carcass, the contact caused a dry, hollow sound. The eyes were dark and milky, with clumps of dried matter surrounding the rim and streaking its face.

Leo had continued lovingly narrating his collection, and

his eyes sparkled with a strange fascination as he waved his hands across the various remains. He had shared the stories of each animal's demise and how he came about them as if they were prized holographic Pokémon cards.

"Then I got this squirrel just last week. Look." Leo took his finger and poked at the stump where the squirrel's tail used to be.

"The car tire snatched it off!" He explained gleefully.

Leo continued joyously describing how he came about each of the rodent corpses until Craven broke into a convulsing cough.

With a wave of nausea threatening to rush up from the pit of his stomach, Craven spun on his heel and ran. Bouncing off the side of the doorway, he propelled himself back down the hall toward the Meetup Station. Claire was still deep in conversation with the therapist but his father was nowhere in sight.

"HE'S GOT DEAD ANIMALS IN HIS BACKPACK, MOM!" Craven yelled as he stumbled into the room, holding his inhaler to his mouth. The counselor began flipping pages on his notepad as Craven turned his attention toward him. "Did you even know about this?"

"Calm down, honey," Claire reached for his arm and he moved back a step to prevent her touch.

"I can't calm down because I can't fucking breathe, Mom! It's not a joke! I'm not overreacting! Have you met me? I have asthma!" Craven's eyes filled with tears, frustrated and overwhelmed with more emotion than he was able to express. He collapsed onto the lounge chair.

"Craven, listen, we actually didn't know about the... the animals until we got here today."

"Dead animals, Mom. They're literally *dead*." Craven repeated.

The therapist had stood and stretched out his hand to Craven.

"I'm Dr. Pharaoh Lindsey – but you can call me Pharaoh. I actually work with your dad, so I like to consider myself a friend. I apologize for not making your acquaintance much sooner, Craven."

Dr. Lindsey was even more of a striking figure when he stood towering over Craven and his mother. With a deep brown complexion and eyes that twinkled with sparks of blue as he smiled, something about him felt overpowering to Craven, yet also inviting. Craven accepted his handshake and immediately calmed.

"The dead pets are his therapy animals. He finds them comforting and they help with his extreme anxiety." Pharaoh glanced at Claire, who nodded as if she understood. "I know it's difficult for us to understand, but Leo has a very unique relationship with death. He doesn't see things the way you and I and the rest of us do. He's quite comfortable with them in their current state."

"This is just weird, man. And he doesn't seem like he'll want to get rid of them, so you're just gonna have to squash this deal and we can start over with a different kid."

"CRAVEN!" Claire interrupted. "Stop it right now. He's not a puppy! Show some respect! He's been through enough already. For goodness sakes, the woman who runs the home just got killed in a horrible accident right out there in the street!"

"He can make new friends," snorted Craven, rolling his eyes. "I had to do it. He can too."

"That's enough. It's not up for discussion," Claire said. "We'll figure it out, but what you're not going to do is make him feel like some sort of monster."

"Perhaps when you guys get Leo home and he's all

settled into his new space, I could drop by and spend some time with everyone together. Just to observe and offer guidance going forward," Pharaoh suggested with his hand on Craven's shoulder.

"How does that sound to you, Craven? Might that help?"

Pharaoh's voice sounded so incredibly soothing that Craven felt the tension begin to leave his body. His muscles relaxed and the anger subsided quickly.

"Hey, Craven, my man, how about we go together and check on Leo?" Pharaoh gestured toward the exit. They passed Paul as he returned, eating from a bag of popcorn.

Claire fell into her husband's embrace, burying her face into his neck.

"Do you think we should have told him that Leo's mother was your patient before she died?" She mumbled into his shoulder. "It might help Craven understand why we want to help Leo."

Paul shook his head. "In due time, honey. We don't want to overwhelm him with too much at once."

EVANGELINE

Nine years earlier, Dr. Paul Bennett stood in the hallway watching his colleague, Pharaoh, facilitate a counseling session with a group of patients. Pharaoh was, as always, amazing to watch as he took control of the room and seemingly lulled the clients into a trance. They hung on his every word and sat listening, eyes wide and completely enthralled. When the other therapists might meet in the break room and moan about feeling ineffective in their roles, Pharaoh seemed to have mastered the magic of finding that connection with his patients.

During their time at the treatment center, he and Paul had become close friends, but Paul often felt more like a fan than a friend. So much so that Claire would jokingly accuse Paul of fangirling over his associate.

"Oh, why don't you just kiss him," she'd gently rib Paul, laughing, whenever he gushed over something Pharaoh had done at work. "You wanna marry him, don't you?" She cracked herself up, but even Paul chuckled a bit because he couldn't deny that Pharaoh was kind of a big deal.

With several years residency before Pharaoh arrived at the clinic, the two men formed an instant connection from the day they bumped shoulders in the lounge area. Paul was immediately struck by Pharaoh's six-and-a-half-foot tall imposing stature and devastatingly good looks. He was both charming and effusive as he flashed a wide grin and jumped back, offering the chair to Paul as his eyes sparkled with good cheer. They continued accidentally bumping into each other throughout the four-story practice until finally Pharaoh invited Paul for a drink after work. They'd been best work buddies ever since, or as Claire liked to tease, work spouses.

Paul was enthralled by the way the men sat almost trance-like in their chairs, smiling and nodding softly, listening to Pharaoh with a rapt attention. Paul longed to command that type of attention from his patients during a group counseling session. Now Pharaoh — a snappy dresser with a signature black newsboy hat cocked to the side - that was a guy that could charm a snake or talk a man down from a ledge.

Distracted by movement, Pharaoh looked over and spotted Paul watching from the observation window. He flashed his signature white and perfect grin, waving his arm in greeting. Turning back to his patients, he fired off a few more magical words and returned ownership of their bodies to them once more. The men visibly loosened their muscles and began moving freely in their chairs, stretching arms and legs as if they had been frozen.

"How's it going, buddy?" Pharaoh stepped into the hallway and wrapped Paul into a big bear hug.

"Just checking out the master at work, as usual! One

day I'm going to learn how to hypnotize people the way you do," Paul joked, playfully throwing a punch at Pharaoh's muscular arm.

"Practice, that's all. You learn what they want most, and then you make them believe you're the only person who can do that for them. Wrapped around your finger, you know, like the song?" Pharaoh grinned again, holding up one finger and twisting it slowly in the air to illustrate his point.

"You think that will work with my kid?"

"Aw, your boy Craven is not so bad. He's a teenager, they hate everybody. You'll be fine. Give it a few years and you won't be able to shake him off of you."

Paul dramatically rolled his eyes. "That's if I survive a few years!"

"Listen, I'm glad you popped by. I've got something for you. This case I was given yesterday, I don't think I can handle it with my current caseload. Wondering if you might want to take it over? She's a referral from the psychiatric hospital," Pharaoh pulled a notepad and pen from his jacket and scribbled some words before handing it to Paul.

"You'd be doing me a big one for this," he said, again with the big smile that no one could decline.

"Sure, I'll take a look. What's the story on her?"

"Well, long story short – she has some issues with reality. About who she is and...*what* she is." Pharaoh chuckled. "You'll find her very interesting, I'm certain!"

Moments later, Paul found himself sitting at his desk reading through the medical file for a 26-year-old black woman named Evangeline Foreman.

. . .

Evangeline entered the system a little more than six months ago, and by way of Pharaoh's referral, her file ended up in Paul's queue.

She was found wandering the streets, disheveled and confused; at times delusional or completely withdrawn.

When onlookers approached her to offer help, she spouted off incomprehensible ramblings about ancient cultures and civilizations; claiming to have lived multiple lives and to be more than 500 years old. A few people tried to get her to into a shelter for safety, either from the elements or from other dangers, but they were soon scared away by her erratic and violent outbursts.

Eventually, she was taken into custody and brought to the psychiatric hospital for observation. At first, she seemed peaceful and compliant. But as the medical staff began to ask her questions, her demeanor quickly changed. She began to chant in a language that none of them could understand. Her voice grew louder and louder as she shouted and gestured wildly. She even went through the motions of putting a curse on the attendants who were responsible for keeping her restrained.

Once subdued and well medicated, she stared at the ceiling, her eyes blazing with anger, murmuring in the same unintelligible dialect.

It would be nearly a year before she was stabilized enough to sit for regular therapy evaluations. The sessions with a doctor could help her uncover the source of her trauma and get her on the road to healing.

The doctor assigned to her was Dr. Paul Bennett.

Months later, Paul Bennett strode down the hallway of the psychiatric wing of the hospital clutching his tablet beneath the crook of his elbow. His stomach twisted and grumbled in knots as he got closer to Evangeline's room for their weekly therapy appointment, and the dim lighting in the hospital didn't help much with his mood. You would think they'd have brighter hues in such a place, he mused as if it was his first time visiting.

On the outside, he was a consummate professional - confident, wise, and on top of his game. On the inside, however, he was a tangled mess of confusion, guilt and shame. His desires would have him cross ethical boundaries, but he couldn't pull himself away from the dark mystery that was Evangeline.

Reflecting back on the first time he evaluated her, she was in the hospital intake room, bewildered and angry, spouting about demons that she swore would soon arrive to avenge her. The fire in her eyes drew Paul in as soon as he stepped to her bedside and Evangeline fixed her stare on his face. This surely wasn't a regular patient, and Pharaoh had to be aware of that, which was why he passed her to Paul.

As time went by, and Paul learned more about her alleged past lives, his curiosity grew louder. Paul would stay up all night researching the occult, trying to understand her background.

A continuous theme in Evangeline's stories was that she was being followed by a tall black man who she couldn't communicate with. Playing back recordings of their sessions, Paul listened for clues and researched specific characters from the black magic realm.

His psychiatric background told him that people who regularly appear in dreams have a definitive link to the dreamer, so he wanted to reassure her that she wasn't entirely off base with her fears. But it would take more gentle nudging into her memories to figure out who he might be. Which meant many more sessions of therapy. That part was okay with him. It would grant him more time in her sweet presence.

If Paul were being honest with himself, he hated his near perfect suburban life. His marriage had become routine, predictable and boring. He felt imprisoned by the expectations of his family, career and community. Where Evangeline was concerned, he got to experience something unconventional. Something that awakened a fire within him. Her unapologetic – albeit delusional - embrace of the occult awoke a danger inside of his own heart.

Even if Paul wanted to stop, cancel her appointments and transfer her to yet another doctor, he couldn't. He couldn't explain it or make sense of it, but he often felt powerless in her presence, as if invisible strings were being pulled, driving his bad decisions.

So, he continued to hide his growing feelings behind his Ivy League credentials - using his medical professional privilege to probe deeper into the mystery of this strange woman.

He promised himself that he wasn't going to back down from the challenge handed to him by his dear friend Pharaoh.

ON THIS DAY, Evangeline entered the room as usual, eyes red and puffy. She greeted Paul with a weak smile, and Paul returned her smile and added a small wave of his hand, immediately feeling silly.

"Idiot! Did you just wave?" He thought as he tucked one hand inside the other.

"Good afternoon, Evangeline," he said, his voice trembling slightly. "I hope you had an easy trip over."

"Easy trip? On the looney tunes van? Sure." She settled into the plush side chair, clutching a tissue in her trembling hands. Her vulnerability tugged at Paul's heartstrings, and he struggled to listen attentively as she began to talk about the days since her last session.

"He's still following me, Dr. Bennett. I know you don't believe he's real. You think he's not really there, but I saw him, I swear!"

"Now...wait, let's try to examine this again. You said before that you'd called the police and they --"

"-- they couldn't locate anyone. They checked the cameras from the businesses along the street, but they didn't see him."

Paul cleared his throat and scribbled a note on her sheet.

"Why do you think that is, Evangeline? If he was there, surely someone would have seen him."

"He doesn't want to be seen. At least, not the way he shows himself to me. He was there," she leaned forward and stared into Paul's face. "He changes into different things when they look for him."

Paul felt a cold chill run up his spine as he met her stare; her lips quivered and the tears rolled down her cheeks as she described the man that had for months haunted her waking dreams. Paul tried to redirect the conversation back to the key points of the path she should be on, but he couldn't resist the temptation to dive deeper into her fears.

"Evangeline," he said softly, "Have you considered that maybe he is just a-a-a figment of your imagination? Maybe representative of something else that's bothering you?"

"I don't know what he wants from me, but I know that if I don't run - if I don't keep running - that I'll die if he catches me!"

She's even more beautiful when she cries.

Paul cleared his throat and reached into the drawer for his prescription pad.

"I can see how much pain you're in. I want to help you, and I think it's time we consider medication as an option. It could provide you with some needed rest, which would help manage your anxiety." He began hastily scribbling a prescription for valium to help her sleep.

Evangeline nodded, tears streaming down her face. "I trust you, Dr. Bennett," she whispered, her voice filled with gratitude.

I trust you.

"But it's not fucking sleep that I need." She stood and walked over the window, pulling back the curtain to look down at the traffic below.

"I suppose if I just let him catch up to me, this will all be over," Her fingers began tapping idly against the window, the short sharp tips of her fingernails made loud clicking sounds on the glass pane.

Paul's hand paused in motion and he looked over at Evangeline's back, outlined by the soft sunlight bathing the window pane. He couldn't explain it, but whenever he was in her presence, she had this irresistible pull over his emotions. Instead of being in control of the sessions, he felt helpless, like he was her puppet and she was the one leading him to say the things she needed him to say; possibly *do* the things she needed him to do. Those things included signing off on whatever clearance she needed to get more freedom on her treatment plan, access to leave her facility several times during the week, for extended periods of time.

Whatever Evangeline asked Paul to do, he felt unable to tell her no.

"Why do you believe that this figure, this man, wants to hurt you? Sometimes dreams have many layers of reality. Maybe he has some information to share with you, related to your past."

"His face, I've seen his face and it's not the face of someone who wants to have a nice little chat." She paused the tapping and instead began tracing a finger across the window pane, dragging a series of arcs and shapes slowly across the glass, then connecting them with lines that only she could see.

"I had a dream about him once. He was standing in the corner, in my room at the shelter. I was too scared to move but I wanted to see his face. I figured if I could stare him down, then maybe that would take away some of his power. So, I sat up and looked directly into the corner and all I could see was his dark shape and these… horns… coming out of his forehead." Evangeline extended her fingers to trace two shorter shapes on the window.

"I'll never forget the horns. They were glistening wet."

A shudder ran down the back of Paul's neck as he listened to the description of an evil figure unlike anything he'd ever heard or read about — and in his profession, he'd heard about a lot of outrageous dreams. Despite under-going shock therapy and dosages of medication that should have neutralized Evangeline's wild tales, she still insisted that what she claimed was, in fact, true.

Their sessions became less about Paul helping Evange-line, and more of her regaling him with stories about some of the demons she had encountered in her many lifetimes. It became quite an odd imbalance of purpose, and Paul knew he had crossed the line when he found himself trying to look up some of the metaphysical spirits she would spin tales about. Instead of helping her heal, he was close to sliding down into the psychotropic rabbit hole along with her.

He considered approaching his mentor, Pharaoh, on the day he felt his heart flutter when Evangeline walked in the room and his face flushed red. He didn't think about Evangeline until she was there, but then suddenly, there would be something undeniably stirred within his soul.

As her therapist, Paul was toe-tapping dangerously close to professional misconduct. When he should have been helping Evangeline navigate her mental health issues, he was supporting her wild fantasies of monsters following her on public streets.

It came as quite a shock when this devoted Anglo-Saxon family man realized he had fallen into something that was wholly unethical, even disgraceful. Still, this woman - correction, this patient - was in his head and it felt less like an obsession than *possession*.

If she had asked him to write her an authorization for release, he would have gladly typed it up and signed it and sent it to the judge. A line was going to be crossed, and Paul knew it was coming, but he was completely under Evangeline's spell and could do nothing to stop it.

THEM BENNETT BOYS

Leo pouted and slumped against the wall; he had been kicked out of the classroom and sent to the hallway. Again. He spent a lot of time there. His teacher joked that she should place a chair there with his name on it. Scrubbing his shoes back and forth on the floor, Leo turned his head and listened to the muffled voices of the teacher discussing his latest episode with Claire.

How many times would he have to explain himself? It wasn't his fault that other kid had fallen down the stairs after he pushed Leo. Leo had barely touched the other kid, and Leo was certain that the cameras in the stairwell would back him up. He didn't have to touch him. Things had a way of happening, sometimes, just because Leo really wanted them to. And he had really wanted that kid to understand what it felt like to be pushed.

But the kids at school found different ways to get a rise out of Leo. To them, he was just the weird foster kid who drew pictures of dead animals and stared too much. Leo was used to getting bumped and shoved each time they had to walk to the lunchroom or head to the gym. But when he started to fight back, then suddenly, it was a problem.

One particular day, he had smuggled Pecan Pie to school in his backpack and managed to keep it hidden until recess. While the other kids played on the field, he found a spot under the slide where he sat and played with the dead rabbit in peace. That was, until a girl named Persia popped her head into his hiding space and started bothering him.

"Ugh! What is that? Is that dead?" Persia had twisted her nose and scrunched her eyebrows, making the ugliest face Leo had ever seen on a girl.

He covered Pecan Pie with his forearm, feeling suddenly defensive.

"YOU PLAYING WITH A DEAD RABBIT?" She shouted, her voice seemed to bounce off the aluminum slide and circled around the playground.

"Shut up, stupid!" Leo hissed. "He's not dead!"

"He sure looks dead to me! Let me see!" She dropped down and crawled into the space, sitting cross legged across from Leo, demanding. "Let me see it!"

Leo had smirked, then slowly scooped up the rabbit and tossed it at Persia's lap. Persia's eyes had widened and she shrieked, pushing herself backwards against the stairs while Leo giggled. Suddenly, Persia had stopped moving and leaned forward, staring at the rabbit on her leg.

"You're right, it's not dead. It's moving," she whispered, poking at its mouth.

Leo watched her contentedly. It was rare that he shared his creatures with anyone else; he was tickled by her reaction as she took her finger and tapped the rabbit's mouth.

"OUCH! He bit me!" Persia cried out as she jumped up from the ground. The rabbit rolled down her legs, landing in the woodchips. Leo tried to stop Persia, but she took off screaming across the field toward the playground monitor who promptly confiscated and then threw the dead rabbit into the trash.

Later that day, that same rabbit tumbled out of Leo's desk, where he'd tried to conceal it long enough to smuggle it back home. So, he found himself back in the hallway, listening to the teacher tell her version of the story.

Leo wasn't too worried about Claire. She treated him with warmth and patience, but he sensed that her good faith might be fading. He longed for the time to come when he could show the world who he really was inside, to let them know he was no ordinary little kid, but something much more powerful. Something to be feared, not ignored or treated like a weird foster kid.

Until then, he would continue to play the game. But some days, it was hard to fight the urge to burst out of his shell.

As a newly ordained big brother, one of Craven's daily duties was to usher Leo back and forth from elementary school. The walk took approximately 20 minutes, but it was the most awkward and uncomfortable 20 minutes of each of Craven's weekdays. The two kids had been living in the same house for several months, but the time they spent alone together still left Craven feeling uneasy and anxious to get away. He simply couldn't connect with Leo, and he couldn't get past the feeling that Leo would erase him completely if possible.

Deep down in his heart, Craven knew that he'd missed his opportunity to bond that day Leo excitedly introduced Craven to his little friends. Craven had let Leo down and Leo would not let him forget it. It was clear now that when

Leo had excitedly presented his road kill collection to Craven – like a housecat displaying a dead mouse to its owner – Craven was supposed to be amazed, plopping down on the bed to play with the little mangled germ-filled pouches. Instead, he had recoiled in disgust, and Leo took the reaction personally.

Craven both shrugged and shuddered at the memory. It still gave him the creeps. His parents should have thrown a flag on the entire adoption that day, as Craven had boldly demanded, but now he stood outside of the elementary school waiting for his *brother* to exit.

Just a few yards from the door, Craven leaned against a tree and observed the children running through the double exit doors. They were so...*childlike*. And, mostly, happy. Like kids. They rushed out into the afternoon, faces turned up to the sun; screaming with joy as they collided with friends or rushed to meet their waiting chaperones and parents.

Their eyes sparkled as they chattered to each other with enthusiasm about what they did in school that day, or what they were planning to do the rest of the day. There was a swirl of energy around the school front as the surge of students darted back and forth on the sidewalk and as supervisors tried to corral them into bus lines, or to angle them toward the crossing guards for their walks home.

And then there was Leo.

The doors closed shut. After a few minutes, one door slowly opened, pushed from the inside, and Leo walked through at his normal leisurely pace.

His face was characteristically blank; expression unreadable. Those daunting brown eyes detached from the cheerful chaos surrounding him as he kept his gaze straight ahead. An older woman – a teacher, perhaps – wearing a badge on a lanyard, was standing closest to the door. She reached out to catch the door as it swung inward, then she held it open so Leo could exit. He walked past without so much as acknowledging her kind gesture with a smile or a nod. Craven imagined that he spotted a bit of a sour smirk on the woman's face as she looked back at Leo before walking into the school.

Leo walked right past the tree where Craven stood leaning, and Craven had to shuffle up next to him and get a few steps in the lead.

"How was school?" He asked, reaching for Craven's old, brightly colored Pokémon themed backpack that his parents insisted Leo take to school, instead of the *Pet Sematary* special one he preferred.

Leo allowed Craven to slip the backpack from his shoulders as they picked up their pace on the sidewalk and headed toward home.

"That good, huh?" Craven snarked.

"I hate everybody," replied Leo, stooping to pick up a random rock that caught his eye. He turned it over in his hands and dusted the dirt off before slipping it into the front pocket of his jeans.

"What happened now?" Craven asked with a frown. Leo simply gave him a scowl and stepped around him, continuing to walk along the sidewalk.

He snickered and mumbled. "You're not the boss of me."

"Why are you collecting rocks anyway? Dumb." Craven took the lead again, but didn't stray so far that he wouldn't hear or sense Leo behind him. If anything happened to Leo, Craven's mom would blame him and probably kick him out to the street.

For some odd reason, this kid was *so stinkin' precious* to her. Wasn't Craven enough? Seriously, what gave?

Craven glanced back to make sure Leo wasn't picking up more sharp, dangerous objects to take home to slaughter the family with in their sleep. They were getting close to their house when he noticed that Leo was walking slowly, and had his head turned toward one of the homes. He was staring up at the front door of the problematic Taylor family house, which was a few doors down from their own home.

Walking quickly in Leo's direction, Craven shouted the boy's name, trying to stop him from approaching the house. Craven saw puffs of smoke floating through the screen door, and as he got closer, he smelled the harsh cigarette fumes. From inside, he heard a man's voice saying something to Leo that he couldn't make out, almost whispering. He looked up and saw the bare-chested, heavily tattooed, and much disliked Joe Taylor, standing inside the door, beckoning to Leo.

"Leo, no." Craven reached for his arm, but Leo jerked away.

"Don't go up there!" Craven hissed under his breath. "Keep walking!"

"Oh, heyyyyyyy there, it's the Bennett boy too!" Joe Taylor turned his attention to Craven. "Hiya doing, Bennett boy? Where's your Pa?"

Craven rolled his eyes and continued whispering to Leo, imploring him to keep along their path and to ignore the man.

"Ya hear me talking to ya?!" The man raised his voice.

"He's at work, I guess," replied Craven, stepping in front of Leo to block him from walking up the steps.

Joe Taylor stepped out onto the porch with his bare feet and dirty sagging jeans.

"At work, huh? He still work at that fancy hospital?"

Craven ignored him.

Joe Taylor and his wife Vicki were the local outcasts whom everyone wanted to get rid of, but no one had the tools to make them leave. The dilapidated house had been their home for many years. The police were often called to break up arguments between the intoxicated lovers, or confrontations with their neighbors about how their out-of-control pit bulls chasing people up and down the street, or complaints of hoarding on their property.

Neither of the Taylors worked, surviving instead of government assistance, most of which was obviously used to pay for alcohol and dog food, judging from the trash strewn about the yard.

At one point in time, Joe and Craven's father had been something like friends. It was many years ago. They'd grown up in the town together and went to all of the same schools. Even played on the sports teams together. But when Paul Bennett went away to college and came home with a respectable career, Joe suffered a series of physical and then financial setbacks that made him what he was today. And, well, like attracts like, so he met Vicky and they laid their roots right there in that house.

However, the collective disdain for this couple went beyond their social or economic status. Their strange behavior over the years lead to whispers and rumors that they may also be involved in things more nefarious. Things that people didn't like to talk about in public because it reminded them of the kind of pure evil that exists in the world.

But without any real proof, the suspicions just became the stuff of local gossip, and residents knew not to invite the pair to any city-wide events. In fact, most folk crossed the street rather than walk past their door and risk being accosted by Joe or his equally-strange looking wife.

However, Leo wasn't familiar with the Taylor's reputation, and Craven had been too distracted to protect him from the harsh introduction he was about to receive.

"Tell your DADDY that I wanna talk to him," said Joe, before spitting a wad of brown-colored tobacco over the porch rail and into the grass. He began dancing a little jig and singing, grinning wildly. "I think I'm a little craaaaaazy! I need to talk to your daddy!"

"What you got there?" His wife Vicki suddenly appeared in the door behind him. She wore a dirty pink tank top over flowered leggings with holes up and down the legs, either from wear, or from moths. Her stringy blonde hair had patches missing where Joe had gotten the better of her during one of their infamous battles. But she stepped out on the porch and grabbed her husband's waist as if he was the love of her life.

From behind, she rested her chin on his shoulder and pointed at Leo, who Craven had managed to stop in his tracks.

"What you got there, a black kid?" Vicki said, her skinny arm hanging in the air, pointing as if he were a thing and not a child with feelings.

"Where'd he come from?" She asked again, louder.

"Come on, Leo. Ignore them. Let's go. Keep walking," Craven stuck his arm out in front of Leo, protectively, and gently nudged him back toward the sidewalk.

"I think that's the kid they adopted! You remember, we heard he was coming," Joe reminded her as she let go of him and began to walk down the steps toward the boys.

"Isn't that something?" Vicki raised her hand to her

forehead to shield the sun as she leaned forward to look closely at Leo.

"Looks a bit like Paul already, huh?" She laughed and turned to her husband, who had resumed his fancy foot-work on the porch.

"Don't you think so? He looks a like a little *brown* Paul," she said, nearly screaming with laughter.

Suddenly, Joe stopped dancing and grabbed his wife's elbow, pulling her toward the porch. Even in his stupor, he threw an apologetic look over his shoulder to Craven and Leo. He whispered angrily into her ear as he forced her up the stairs and into the door; she tried to resist, but managed one final glance at the boys before Joe pulled her inside and slammed the door. Perhaps even a lifetime loser like Joe had his limitations.

Leo glared at the Taylors screen door with his lips stretched open in a chilling grin. But once they went back inside with the door closed, the spell had been broken. This time, Leo allowed Craven to lead him away. Back on the sidewalk, Leo shrugged out of Craven's hand, preferring to walk behind.

"Drunk bitch," muttered Craven. He turned to Leo and placed a hand on his shoulder. "Don't let her bother you, no one likes her. I'm sorry you even had to meet her."

"Drunk bitch," Leo repeated, and let out a soft giggle.

Craven smiled. It felt good to hear Leo laugh some-times. He may have been a tough kid to love, but Craven wasn't going to let anyone hurt him.

CRAVEN'S SLEEP was wrecked by the piercing sound of sirens and red and blue lights bouncing around his bedroom walls. He jolted upright, shaking off the fuzziness while dashing to the window. Peeking outside, Craven had to turn his head slightly to the right, but he could make out the silhouettes of police cars surrounding the Taylor house. The glow of those headlights struck a nervous chord in Craven's heart.

Cops had been there before, and often, but somehow, this felt and looked more urgent. Craven could see dozens of dark figures moving around in the street as neighbors flooded their lawns; awakened from sleep, they came out wearing robes, pajamas, nightgowns or whatever they could toss on in a hurry to see what was going on.

Unease tightened Craven's chest as he pondered the possibilities, a rush of scenarios, each more unsettling than the last. Did a drunken Joe finally slap Vicki upside the head a little too hard? Did Vicki get fed up with Joe and decide to sweeten his brown liquor with a little antifreeze?

As he continued watching through the blinds and imagining the wildest of crimes, he saw the white coroner's van arrive and back into the Taylor's driveway. The bold, illuminated Coroner decal stood out boldly, even from the distance, and the lights from the patrol cars helped highlight the seriousness of its arrival.

This was much more than a drunken fight.

Craven needed to go see it up close.

Retrieving his inhaler from his bedside table, Craven took a couple of puffs to prepare for the shock of the night air on his lungs, then slipped the device into the pocket of his sweatshirt. Using the light from his cell phone, he scrambled around his room for slippers and a sweatshirt so he could stand outside and gawk with the rest of the street. He poked his head into Leo's room to see if he wanted to wake up and tag along for the circus, but Leo's bed was empty.

By the time Craven made it outside, it seemed the entire street was awake and trying to get a look at the action. They leaned on their cars, sat on their porches, and some had even walked right up to the police barrier so they could get the closest look as someone – dead or alive – was brought out of the house.

Craven pushed his way through the crowd until he was at the yellow tape just a few feet from the edge of the front yard. From where he stood, he could make out bloody footprints across the porch and down the stairs, leading into the grass, where they seemed to stop in one wide patch of blood, clumps of grass, and mud.

"Pretty cool, right?"

A tiny voice spoke softly from the side of Craven's arm. Craven looked down and to the right to find Leo standing there in his pajamas, barefoot. He wasn't wearing a jacket, and although his eyes twinkled with excitement, he appeared cold and his teeth chattered lightly when he smiled.

"How did you get here before me? Why didn't you wake me up? Where's your coat?" Craven surprised himself by launching into big brother mode, but standing outside of a bloody crime scene might understandably have that effect on a kid.

Leo stretched his arms upward, silently begging Craven to lift him off the ground.

Without hesitation, Craven turned and kneeled so that his back faced Leo, in the universal symbol of "hop on."

Leo wrapped his tiny arms around Craven's neck and brought his legs up so Craven could grab them and lift him safely.

He was much lighter than Craven thought he would be, even for an 8-year-old. Leo slid his hands inside of the front neckline of Craven's hoodie to get warm, and although Leo's fingers were cold against his skin, Craven felt a twinge of comfort knowing that he had him on his back.

Craven reached down and guided Leo's small feet into the pockets on each of the sweatshirt and he heard Leo giggle.

They stood and watched the police swarm the house, looking for evidence and clues, while the attendants from the coroner's office began to make their way down the front steps with a pair of stretchers.

On top of each stretcher was a zipped and sealed body bag, secured with straps to hold them in place as they descended the stairs.

Craven recognized the voices of his neighbors standing behind him in the dark, discussing what they knew, or thought they knew, about the apparent murders of the Taylors. Craven stood still so he could eavesdrop on the conversation, but what he heard sent chills through his body.

"I heard there wasn't much left to go in those bags."

"Yikes. What do you think happened? Did they take some meth and just go at each other?"

"Don't know for certain but the first cop that came outside, he hurled up his guts right over the railing there!"

"Are you serious? It must be pretty bad if it shook him up!"

"Yessirreee it is! I heard one of the detectives talking on the phone and he said they was torn apart!"

"That kind of thing doesn't happen in this neighborhood!"

"Well, they never really belonged here anyway!"

Suddenly, the crowd got quiet, then a wave of reactions rolled through the air as they expressed surprise and shock.

Craven - who had turned to face the crowd so he could

catch the whispers – noticed everyone had stopped talking and were now staring and pointing toward the crime scene.

He turned and saw a female police officer gently leading a young girl out of the front door by her arm. She was painfully thin, wearing a short, grungy looking sheath dress and flip flops; her hair had been cruelly chopped short, and she covered her face with her hands out of either shame or fear.

The officer raised her hand and signaled to one of the others, who quickly retrieved a plastic wrapped bundle from a nearby patrol car and rushed up the stairs, handing it to her. She ripped off the plastic and shook out a warm wool blanket, gently wrapping it around the girl's head to cover her in privacy, and around her body to keep her warm. The officer then guided the girl down the stairs to another officer who took her hand and led her to one of the cars.

A rumble moved through the crowd as the onlookers gasped and narrated the events unfolded in front of their eyes.

"Who is that?"

"Is that her?"

"Look, there's a kid!"

The officer was now guiding another small child - not much larger than a toddler - out the door and down the stairs. This time, the same woman stacked several packages on the porch and began opening each one and shaking out the blankets and helping to cover and protect each child as one by one, children of varying ages were brought out, wrapped in warm blankets, and placed into the backseats of the patrol cars. The sirens were turned back on and a few of the cars pulled away from the scene. The victims wore tattered and dirty clothing; clearly in distress as they were confronted with bright flashing police lights and a crowd of people recording with their cell phones. Craven counted seven kids before the officer, with tears streaming down her cheeks, sat down on the steps and covered her face with her hands.

"This is so shocking. I don't think I want to live here anymore!"

"At least those kids are safe now!"

"Who would have known this was happening?"

"I knew it! I told y'all there was something strange going on over there!"

At 14, Craven didn't completely understand what had just happened, but from the drastic condition of the children and the outrage rippling through the crowd each time the door opened, he knew it was something horribly sinister. And despite the apparent massacre of the Taylors, he felt a little bit grateful that whatever happened had freed those poor kids from some kind of hell on the other side of the door.

"Let's go home, fellas," His dad had come outside in his robe to search for them.

There was an unsettling vibe in the night air, and when Craven felt his father's firm touch on his elbow, he felt relieved to turn and see his father's face.

Paul smiled and patted Leo on his back with one hand, then turned to usher his kids away from the scene; his other hand outstretched to gently part the onlookers.

Paul, Craven, and Leo walked silently back to the security and safety of their own home, nodding in greeting to a few of the neighbors they passed along the way. Once inside, Craven watched as his father locked the door – something he didn't usually feel the need to do.

"We'll talk about this in the morning. I know you have

some questions, and so do I," Paul assured them both. "I'll see what I can find out and I'll try to help you both understand it all."

They said goodnight and headed to their respective rooms. Craven carried Leo to his room on his back and lowered him onto his twin bed. Knowing that Leo had just trusted him enough for a piggyback ride home, Craven didn't want to ruin the moment by saying the wrong thing. After all, that was a major development in their relationship and he felt a little warm and fuzzy inside.

Instead, he tapped his knuckles lightly against Leo's shoulder after he sat him down, then he turned and left the room without uttering a word, closing the door behind him. Walking back to his room, Craven broke into a slight smile, wondering what their walks to and from school might look like for the next few days.

He had a glimmer of hope that they would finally be able to walk side by side, laughing and talking like the other kids along the same route did. Because, frankly, he was getting tired of looking like he was some type of security guard escorting Leo to school and having to walk three feet ahead.

Standing in his dark bedroom, Craven reached into his sweatshirt pocket to put the inhaler back in the nightstand. His fingers felt something wet and sticky around the hard plastic of the inhaler and for a moment, he worried that it may have somehow cracked and leaked some of the pressurized medication. He pulled the string to the bedside lamp and sat on the bed to examine the inhaler.

In the palm of his hand, the device was covered in blood along with bits of dirt and grass. Stunned and confused, Craven reached into the opposite pocket with his other hand and felt the same dampness, withdrawing his hand to see the same bloody evidence all over his fingertips.

Craven's mind raced as he tried to comprehend what he was seeing and why? How? Craven sat and stared at his hands, at the inhaler, going over every possible scenario in his head. He wondered if having his sleep interrupted was making him delirious and paranoid. Any explanation was better than the one that was nagging at him from the corner of his brain. One that involved Leo, because...he just *couldn't.*

Craven tiptoed back down the hall to the bathroom and washed his hands with soap. He had a backup inhaler, so he rinsed the blood off the soiled one and tossed it into the wastebasket.

Things would look different in the morning with a clear head.

As Craven passed Leo's room, a soft beam of moonlight from his window escaped beneath his door. Matching shadows – like tiny feet – moved quickly to the side, away from Leo's approach.

Craven's breath caught in his throat and he quickened his pace to his room. He locked his door from the inside and ripped off the soiled sweatshirt, tossing it over in the corner. When he finally climbed back into his bed, he pulled the covers over his head and lay there, trembling, until he fell asleep.

Morning sounds.

Chatter from the downstairs kitchen.

Something frying on the stovetop, cabinet doors opening and closing.

Craven was groggy and the space behind his eyes

throbbed painfully from a lack of sleep. All night, his eyes had stayed open, trying to peer between the fabric of his blanket to keep an eye on his bedroom door. He had been too scared to drift off, even as the moonlight faded and the morning sun shone through the blinds.

A short time after he'd climbed back into bed, Craven had thought he heard Leo shuffling around in his own room. There was the sound of a zipper, a rustle of items dropping to the floor, and then Leo whispering quietly, but forcefully.

Craven had sat up in the bed to listen closely. It was unmistakable. Leo was having a conversation with himself, or with...*someone*. But he could hear words being spoken, lots of words, and there was no one in the room except Leo.

Now that Craven could hear his parents starting their mornings, he felt it was finally safe to come out from under the blanket and to leave the room.

Turning the knob slowly, Craven opened his bedroom door and made sure the coast was clear before tiptoeing over to the bathroom. He tried to keep his movements silent, but the noise of turning the squeaky faucet handle and subsequent running water was anything but quiet. He hastily got dressed in the damp bathroom and nearly stumbled into Leo, blocking the doorway on the other side.

"Uh, sorry – excuse me," Craven mumbled, turning sideways to slide past. Leo was already dressed and stood in his way, holding his dead pet backpack in one hand.

Leo grinned and held up his arms to be picked up again.

"What the hell - NO!" Craven jumped back and bumped into the wall. "What are you doing?"

Disappointed, Leo dropped his arms and turned away, heading toward the stairs, and dragging the backpack behind him. Craven waited for Leo to descend the stairs, wincing as the bag made a thud on each step. He shuddered at the thought of the corpses inside jostling about and breaking into a mass of random, dried out pieces.

"Well, good morning, boys!" Claire rushed to the stairs and embraced a stiffened Leo first, then Craven as he followed behind.

"Pretty rough night. Are you okay? You wanna talk about it?" Paul asked as he pulled their chairs out from the table and beckoned them to sit down. "Leo, you know what we agreed on – the backpack stays away. Not at the table, please."

Claire frowned. "What happened to the other backpack? You know you can't take *that one* to school."

She pointed at the bag on the floor next to the kitchen table.

Leo rolled his eyes. "I just brought them down so they could get some air."

"Okay, as long as you put them somewhere... safe... before leaving for school." She reached out to tousle his curls and Leo shrugged her hand away.

Paul poured himself a cup of coffee and sat at the table while Claire sat cereal bowls in front of Craven and Leo.

"I've been trying to get more information about what happened down the street, to Joe and Vicki," Paul said as he cleared his throat and pondered how much the boys really needed to know. They had witnessed the aftermath of the raid, and the danger was over at this point, but they would certainly have questions.

"The police aren't saying much right now, procedure and all. But it looks like they were, uh..."

"They were stealing kids?" Leo asked innocently over a spoonful of frosted flakes.

"What? Who – what do you mean?"

"The kids. Did they steal them?"

"That's part of, well, that's part of the investigation that we aren't being told about yet. But it looks like the kids are all safe now, and they're being reunited with their parents," said Paul.

"That's good. Sometimes bad things have to happen so the good things can happen next," Leo said with a gleam in his eye. "Right, Craven?"

"Did they say anything about what actually happened to them?" Craven asked, keeping his eyes on his bowl and shoveling cereal into his mouth.

"It wasn't good, son. Something really violent took place inside that house. Maybe they finally got so high that they went at each other to the end. But I'll say this much – it's gonna be quite a job for the coroner to... put back together," Paul looked over at Leo as he carefully chose his words.

"So, were they all chewed up or something?" Leo asked, grinning.

"Okay, that's enough," Claire interrupted. "Let's hold off on this until we know more. You boys have to get to school."

Craven was relieved when they started their walk and a small group of kids happened to be walking at the same time. That would eliminate him having to be alone with Leo for a while. He still felt queasy about the memory of the blood and the grass in his pocket and, try as he might, he couldn't shake the feeling that Leo had something to do with the Taylor's unfortunate ending.

And if he did, well, Craven certainly didn't want to get on his bad side.

OTHER SUGARY DELIGHTS

Paul steered the car through the quiet suburban streets, while Leo sat silently in the passenger seat, his gaze fixed on the passing scenery. He'd ditched music from the start of the drive, after not being able to connect his phone to the car's Bluetooth, so their tune of choice for the journey was the wind whipping against the car on the highway. Paul stole glances in Leo's direction and tried to break the heavy silence that had enveloped the inside of the car.

"Excited for some ice cream, Leo?" Paul asked, trying to inject a sense of warmth into the air. Leo nodded, shyly, a faint smile flickering on his lips.

"Look, Leo," Paul cleared his throat, searching for the words. "I-I know we haven't spent much time together, just you and I. I'm sorry for that. I feel I owe you a little extra time, since I knew Evangeline – your mother – I knew her well."

From the corner of his eye, Paul saw Leo turn his head to look at him; felt him staring into the side of his face. He kept his eyes on the road and, after a few moments, Leo looked away. An icy chill ran up the center of Paul's spine.

This kid.

He didn't exactly light up rooms when he walked in, and that was fine and to be expected. He'd been through a lot. He'd lost his mother during childbirth, then grown up on the move, shuffled from one foster home to the next. But there was a cold, distant demeanor to Leo that Paul couldn't seem to crack, not even with all his professional degrees, licensing and training.

"I'm really sorry, Leo," Paul added softly. "Your mother was a wonderful person and she had so much to share with the world. She-"

"With you?" Leo interrupted him.

"Huh?"

"Did she share a lot with you?" Leo turned those cold eyes again in Paul's direction, staring, waiting for his response.

"We-we spent a lot of time together in her sessions. I-I was her counselor, and yes, well-yes, she shared a lot with me about her life, her past-"

"That's not what I mean and you know it, Paul."

Paul opened and closed his mouth rapidly, soundlessly. He didn't know how to respond, or if he should. This was a delicate time and Evangeline was a delicate topic. He wanted to give Leo space to adjust, but he also wanted to set boundaries and expectations in light of the previous challenges he knew the boy had suffered at other homes.

How long are you gonna pussyfoot around the truth?

He stole a glance in Leo's direction and felt relieved that Leo had returned to staring out the window.

It certainly won't be today.

They would talk about Evangeline eventually. But not today.

The ice cream shop came into view as they came down the exit ramp; a quaint little place with a colorful sign beckoned them to continue forward to the parking lot. Paul parked the car and as they stepped out into air filled with the sweet aroma of waffle cones and other sugary delights.

The inside of the ice cream parlor was lively with more than half of the booths occupied by customers who were engaged in conversations over their ice cream treats. Paul quickly scanned the room and took in the smiling families. He wondered wistfully if he and Leo might sit in a booth together and share a laugh or two over a couple of sundaes like the rest of them.

A gray-haired heavyset man moved around behind the counter, adjusting the buckets of frozen treats and wiping down the knives that were used to carve and chop the solid blocks of cream on the wooden board. Now in his late sixties, Clarence had seen a lot of things. And from what Paul could tell, Clarence tended to like even less things the more he saw. Crossing his arms, Clarence scowled and watched through slitted eyes as Paul and Leo approached his counter.

"Afternoon!" Paul greeted him and peered through the glass cases, taking in the rows of ice cream tubs, fixings, and toppings. "Wow, everything looks so good. How do you choose?"

Clarence grunted and shrugged, continuing to wipe down the counters without glancing up. "You just pick one," he muttered.

"Leo, buddy, what are you thinking? Cone or sundae?" Paul turned and lightly, affectionately tapped Leo's shoulder.

Leo allowed himself a rare opportunity to loosen up and stepped closer to study the flavors. Rocky road with marshmallows looked fun, but so did cookies and cream. And was peanut butter swirl as delicious as it sounded? His nose pressed up against the case, fogging the glass as he noisily inhaled.

"Hey, no breathing on the glass!" Clarence barked. "You're making it all unsanitary – back up! I just cleaned!"

Paul was alarmed at the sudden and unnecessary change in the clerk's tone. "Was that necessary? He's a kid, for chrissakes!"

Paul looked past Clarence toward the back of the business to see if there were other employees that might step in and take their order.

"It's okay," Leo said, taking a small step back and pointing. "The ones in the back, there, what are those?"

Clarence tossed his rag down angrily. "Look, kid, I don't have time to explain every item to you. Just pick your ice cream so we can keep this line moving."

There were less than a dozen customers standing patiently behind Paul and Leo; Paul looked around at their shocked and confused faces as they witnessed the tense exchange.

"Are you the owner? If not, I'd like to speak to the owner. This is unacceptable. You're being rude to a child for no reason!" Paul pulled out his cellphone to look up the store's website.

Unaffected by Paul's threat, Clarence rolled his eyes and continued to glare at Leo. "Place your order and go, please."

Leo stepped forward with a smile on his face. He tapped Paul on his arm and looked up, beaming.

"It's okay, DAD," he said loudly. "I know what I want."

Turning back to Clarence, he chuckled. "Sorry for taking

so long. I guess I'll have chocolate. With brownie bites. Please."

Leo added, showing his teeth.

"Cone or cup?" Clarence asked, now in a bored voice.

"Cone, please."

Paul was taken aback at Leo's pleasant demeanor, especially in the midst of the clerk's terrible treatment. Leo may be willing to live and let live, but Paul was not going to let the tense exchange go so quickly. Paul confirmed and repeated Leo's order, quickly holding up two fingers to indicate a duplicate for himself, then continued to scroll the store's website looking for a way to contact the owner or leave a review.

The customers in line began to murmur amongst themselves, clearly uncomfortable with what they were witnessing.

Clarence sighed and reached into the display cooler for a block of the selected ice cream. He slammed the frozen square onto the wooden board, then grabbed the chopping knife in his right hand. Leo moved directly in front of the cooler so he could watch his order being prepared. Defiantly, he pressed his face against the glass, grinning, with his hands splayed out on each side of his face.

Clarence raised the knife high in the air and his arm suddenly froze; he began trembling. His mouth opened and closed repeatedly, but no words escaped. His eyes widened and the hand holding the knife began to twitch before it swung wildly, arching toward his shaking body.

"Waaaaaa! Waaaa!" Clarence wailed with a strange, sorrowful tone, throwing back his head, and stumbling backwards until he slammed into the back counter.

A voice from the line cried out, "He's having a stroke! Help him!"

Paul looked up from his phone and jumped into action. Clarence held the knife in the air, twitching wildly as if he were fighting with an invisible attacker. Frantic, Paul looked along the counter for an opening so that he could get behind it to assist the older man. Seeing no other way, he knocked the jars of candy over and hopped across the counter, throwing his legs to the floor on the other side.

"Wahhhhhh!" Clarence gurgled and swung the knife down violently, plunging it into his own stomach. He withdrew the blade, swung it into the air at a sharp angle, and then swiftly brought it back down into his torso.

Screams filled the air as customers cried out. They covered the eyes of their children as they fled the horrific scene. Paul retreated back over the counter to grab Leo, who stood still at the glass case, watching calmly as Clarence mutilated himself with the ice cream knife. His right arm wielded the blade as a weapon, savagely butchering his left, until he collapsed into a pool of blood.

The grin never left Leo's face as Paul pulled him away from the carnage and out the door towards their car.

LINES IN SAND

Although it had been quite shocking, the traumatic accident at the ice cream shop broke new ground for Paul and Leo's burgeoning relationship. Months later, an investigation ruled it to be the result of the poor old man suffering a mental break. As a therapist, Paul looked forward to helping Leo process the event and he hoped it would tighten their bond.

By that point, Leo and Craven had settled into a comfortable arrangement that suited them both. It amounted to, stay out of each other's way and no one would get hurt. Which was pretty typical of boys, whether they were blood-related or not; whether one was suspected of being a murderous psychopath or not.

It was perfectly fine with Craven that they kept their distance, until he spotted Leo walking through the house, dragging a baseball bat around which Craven was sure he remembered hiding in the basement. But that was surely impossible since the trunk was locked and securely tucked away beneath the stairs.

Craven's suspicions were confirmed when he followed closely behind Leo and, sure enough, he caught him disappearing into the basement.

"What are you doing with that?" Craven yelled, and he sprinted the length of the room to snatch his baseball bat from Leo's hands.

The trunk lay with the lid open at Leo's feet, the objects scattered about the inside as if Leo had been rifling through them.

Craven dropped to his knees and searched the trunk to see if anything was missing. Although his own memory was not quite reliable about the contents, he knew that Leo must have bothered something.

"How did you even get it open? You better not have busted the lock! Mommmmm!" Craven pulled the lid over and examined it, scrolling the number dials up and down to see if they were cracked or tampered with, but they seemed to be intact. Leo stared silently at his back.

"You're not gonna talk?" Craven pushed him hard in his chest with both hands. Leo stumbled backwards and fell on his butt, but he never changed his expression. That same flat, menacing stare never left his face, and Leo's eyes remained fixed on Craven as he pushed himself up from the floor.

"MOMMMMM!"

Leo brushed past their mother as she descended the stairs to see what the commotion was about.

"He's been in my stuff! He broke into my trunk, look!"

Claire stopped on the bottom step and crossed her arms, staring accusingly at her oldest son.

"For heaven's sake, they're just old toys. Why can't he play with them? I don't know why you hid them down here in the first place," she began, shaking her head.

In a rush of anger, Craven opened his mouth to present a defense, until he felt the familiar strings of asthma begin to pull at his chest. He reached into his front pants pocket, but came up empty, then felt for the inhaler in his back pocket. It wasn't there either.

Claire continued to fuss at Craven about being selfish, and she ignored the look of panic on her eldest son's face as he realized he didn't have his inhaler close by. Craven kicked the trunk as hard as he could to get Claire's attention and she jumped, startled.

"I need my inhaler!"

Leaping into action, Claire turned and bolted up the stairs, but Leo slunk down in her absence. He took a seat and watched as Craven spun around in circles, trying to calm himself down. Upstairs, Claire frantically pulled out kitchen drawers, searching, rushing back and forth through the house while yelling, "where is it, honey?! I can't find one! Oh my God, where are they?"

Craven contemplated running up the stairs to look for the inhaler himself, but he didn't feel he had the strength to make it.

"Help me...please," he pleaded with Leo, who appeared to be unmoved by Craven's plight. He slid down a little closer to Craven, leaning over to place the back of his hand on the bottom step, opening his fingers wide to release what he was holding.

Out of the corner of his eye, Craven caught a glimpse of a small white object tumbling down the stairs. He heard the clatter of it striking each step on the way down.

Clink. Clink. Clank.

Craven's inhaler hit the floor at his feet.

He dove for it, grasping it in his hand before his chest hit the cold floor; he snatched off the cap and gave it a few quick shakes before puffing it into his lungs. When his body relaxed and he felt strong enough to roll over, Craven turned toward the stairs to find that Leo had slipped away just as quietly as he'd appeared.

"I still can't find any of your inhalers! Do we need to call 911?" Claire yelled down the stairs in a panic.

"It's okay, Mom," Craven replied weakly. "I found it."

"Oh good, sweetie!"

He imagined her happily returning to her chores with a beaming Leo by her side, distracting her from the fact that he'd nearly killed her only child.

Craven pulled himself into a sitting position, keeping his eyes on the stairs. He tuned his ears to the footsteps that crossed the floor above him, and he tried to determine if his mother was alone in the kitchen, or if Leo was nearby. He couldn't stay in the basement forever, but the look in Leo's eyes when he rolled the inhaler down the stairs made him feel that upstairs wasn't the safest place to be either.

Leo had already *possibly* killed the Taylors, so it wasn't beyond Craven's imagination that he would have no qualms about taking him out too. Something had to be done about that kid. Craven didn't know how, but Leo had to go back to where he came from.

THINGS CHANGE

To the casual observer, Evangeline must have looked like a raving lunatic, carrying on about spirits and demons following her through the streets. But her madness stemmed from trauma inflicted by forces beyond anything one could imagine.

At one point in her life – in one of her lives – she had been an impressionable 21-year-old art student and scholar, with a particularly deep interest in ancient books and artifacts. She would spend hours each day in her little bedroom studio sketching and then painting the lush, but often dark, murals in her mind. Her imagination filled in the holes left by the books she translated, and the relics she held in her hands, which only told parts of the history.

Digging deeper for answers led her into studies of the occult. Its connections to the strange and beautiful remnants of broken clay, and its ties to fragile yellowed pages of ancient books. Somehow, Evangeline's path always led back to her own family.

There were segments of her memory that came up

empty. Long periods of time which she couldn't account for, but her childhood had been spent in a multitude of orphanages across the African continent, so it wasn't exactly uncommon to have holes in her knowledge of her background. At first, the whispers in her mind had been inspiring, fueling Evangeline's creative visions.

But her relentless digging for more info finally drew the attention of an entity that wanted to help her to remember, wanted to be seen in its full glory. And when it showed its teeth to Evangeline one night, she didn't shrink in fear because she had recognized it.

His name was Pharaoh and he was her brother.

Not the kind of brother that you grow up with in the same house, sharing cereal, playing in the yard and walking to school. No, Evangeline's brother was born from the same unholy union as herself, several centuries before.

There were many of them spread across the world, tethered to others they may have never spoken to, but who felt their presence all around them anyhow. The powerful male siblings were tasked with guarding and protecting the women as they grew into their purpose. Yet they watched from a distance, while using their magic to manipulate and to control the environment around the women. To keep them safe.

A regal and imposing figure, Pharaoh was both Evangeline's astral guardian and her teacher, watching and following from a distance, but also just a whisper away. After a while, Pharaoh's stalking presence made Evangeline afraid, and she couldn't explain why. He wouldn't — couldn't – harm her, but he began to feel threatening all the same.

They had a silent understanding, no need for words. It had been revealed to Evangeline in a dream that she had a purpose to fulfill before she would finally be able to rest in this life. That purpose was to give birth to the child that would be the catalyst behind some of the most remarkable events known to mankind.

When she landed under Dr. Bennett's care, it wasn't immediately clear that her doctor was also under Pharaoh's influence. But Evangeline noticed how his tone changed over time, and how he showed a willingness to go along with anything she suggested, no matter the ethical risks. Dr. Bennett went from being detached and robotic, making notes on his pad and watching the clock, to being completely enthralled with her stories and showing up to their sessions with folders full of his own research.

Evangeline rubbed her growing belly as she thought about the magnitude of what was going to happen within the next few months. This path had been laid out for her ages ago, and now Pharaoh's mission was clear. Her child would step into his inheritance, and Evangeline would close her eyes one last time. It was a huge responsibility and the pregnancy was taking a heavy toll on her body. Living hundreds of years was apparently a piece of cake, but playing host to a growing, twisting, and turning half-human? Now that was a challenge. But Evangeline was ready to fulfill her purpose.

WITH BOTH BOYS in school during the days, Claire had a chance to sit within her thoughts and reflect on the recent expansion and changes to her family. She hummed softly to herself as she prepped items for dinner. It was a thrill to have the house to herself throughout the day. The isolation allowed her to decompress from all of the movement in and around her life. There was a certain peace in being able to straighten and clean and adjust her home the way she desired, without any input from the rest of the people that lived there.

My house, my rules, she giggled as she fluttered around plucking the items of men from each room. Paul's shoes, Craven's baseball mitt, Leo's rock, random things that irritated her soul to see disturbing the aesthetic of her home.

Speaking of things that disturb the aesthetic, Claire mused as she held one of the rocks in her hand and thought of Leo.

Going in, she accepted that adopting Leo would be a big adjustment for everyone, requiring a little grace on all sides. But with each passing day she found herself questioning if she had made the right decision by bringing Leo into their home. Her cheerful exterior was starting to crack, and her heart stirred a bit of resentment. She had given up her dream of being a teacher in order to marry Paul and raise Craven. But now her life was consumed by housework and managing the lives of not one, but two kids.

And since bringing him into their household was her bright idea, she had no leverage to complain.

Leo was a tough one to warm up to, that was for sure, and his transition to this forever home wasn't going as easy as Claire had convinced herself that it would.

One part of her had hoped that adopting Leo would help bring some life back into their stale family dynamic. But another part of her couldn't let go of the nagging bitter memories of Paul's betrayal.

All of those nights he worked late, tending to poor Evangeline's emotional needs, claiming that he was documenting her mental state and making sure she had the resources she needed to rebuild her life. He was so devoted to his job and to his patients.

Especially this one.

Claire had to laugh when she remembered how Paul walked around believing he had some kind of secret, like he was getting one over on her.

Did he really think she was that stupid?

Or, wait, did he really think he was that smart?

He may be the one with the Ph.D. but Claire was truly the brains of their marriage. The whole time Paul thought he was getting away with something, but Claire knew about Evangeline. She knew about all of the times he had violated, not only his Hippocratic Oath, but also his marriage vows.

The sheer audacity of it all.

Claire had wanted to have another child after Craven, but his birth had been so high-risk that another pregnancy would be far too dangerous. But big, bad, Paul Bennett was out there spreading himself around and getting another woman pregnant – a patient, no less. He had put everything they had built together at risk, simply because he couldn't control himself.

Claire had learned about Leo when Evangeline died during labor, and the baby immediately became a ward of the state. Evangeline had no living or known family, and there had been very little information available about her own history.

For years after, Claire had tracked the little boy's movements through the foster system, noting when he transitioned from one home to another. But somehow no one ever moved to finalize an adoption. Tragedy seemed to naturally follow Leo wherever he went. A series of unfortunate accidents befell the other children and the foster parents, including the horrifying fatal mishap of the administrator at his last temporary home. The poor kid just seemed to have nothing but bad mojo from the day he was born.

All things considered, what Claire didn't want to do was to wait until Leo was old enough to show up on their doorstep, demanding a paternity test, and throwing their entire world into a tailspin. Claire's plan was to take the bull by the horns and to make him part of the family.

What's that saying, keep your enemies close? It would ensure that she knew where he was at all times.

And when the time was right, she would make sure that little Leo was no longer a threat to their perfect family.

LATER THAT AFTERNOON as she cleared the table from breakfast, Claire caught a whiff of that putrid backpack that Leo had promised to put away. It was bad enough that they had to accept this little *handicap* and had to live with a bunch of rotting animals in the house, but the least the kid could do was keep the toxic bag out of their sight.

Sniffing the air, Claire walked around the house, looking for the source of the stench. She found the bag behind the sofa in the living room; wedged into the small open space between the back of the sofa and the wall.

How in the world did he think no one would notice it?

Claire sighed and tugged at the backpack until she was able to pull it out of the tight crevice.

"Yuck!" She covered her nose with one hand and held the bag with her outstretched arm. The sharp corner of a book of some sort peeked out of the zippered pocket on the front of the bag. Curiously, she pulled at the zipper and further opened the pouch to discover an old leather-bound journal filled with lined pages of painstakingly neat, cursive, handwriting. The lines and flourishes were too well developed to have been penned by Leo, but as she carefully flipped through the yellowed pages, she realized that she was holding in her hands the very intimate secrets of Leo's mother, Evangeline.

Claire imagined the woman scribbling her every thought into this book, possibly revealing where she had been, what she had seen, what she had done. As she turned the pages, her heart beat faster with excitement.

This book was the key to Leo's existence! And to think that he had it within his hands all this time. That meant that he knew much more than he was letting on.

The low rumbling sound of the garage door opening and closing signaled that Paul was making a mid-day pit stop at home. Under other circumstances, she might be annoyed at him disturbing her peace, instead, she was bursting at the seams with excitement at the discovery of the journal.

"Paul! Get in here now!" Claire yelled through the house. She carried the book and the backpack into the kitchen where she found her husband searching through the cabinet for a snack.

"Look what I just found in Leo's backpack of death."

She tossed the journal on the table and faced Paul with her hand on her hip.

"What's that?"

Claire tilted her head and looked him in the eye.

"Well, I don't know, I haven't read it yet – but it sure looks like it's his mother's journal! Did you know your *patient* had a journal, Paul?"

Paul's face displayed a mixture of shock, confusion and embarrassment, as he ran through a range of emotions within seconds.

"Yeah, exactly," added Claire, watching warily for his

reaction. Unspoken words hung in the air; they both knew the magnitude of what was in the pages of the book.

"I'm going to put this backpack away – the smell is making me sick to my stomach. When I come back, we can look at this together."

Claire picked up the backpack and headed for the basement. She opened the door and paused at the landing, formulating another thought she wanted to share with her husband. She turned her head just in time to catch the leer of Paul's face as he rushed toward her with his hands raised; before she could release the gasp from her throat, his hands slammed into the small of her back, propelling her down the flight of stairs.

Claire died when her head struck the first step. But her instant demise was a blessing that kept her from feeling the snap of her neck as her body somersaulted the rest of the way down the stairs.

SWEATING PROFUSELY, Paul paced back and forth at the top of the stairs, trying to think of his next move. None of this was according to plan, and thinking fast on his feet was not his strong suit.

Who even knew that woman had been writing in a journal?

He was her therapist and she never once mentioned it to him!

Paul pounded his fist against his thigh as he stood at the top of the stairs, looking at his wife's broken body where it lay on the landing like an abandoned doll. It hurt to see her that way, but Paul would rather his wife die in delusion than let her open that book to learn the truth about how he had betrayed her trust. It would have destroyed her faith in him, his reputation in the community, and everything they had built together.

"Claire, baby, whyyyyyy? Why did you make me do this to you? To us?" Paul cried out to her as she lay crumpled on the floor.

None of this would have happened if she hadn't insisted on adopting Leo and bringing him home. None of it. If only she had left everything alone. But that was Claire. Once she got something in her head, there was no backing her down.

The room was spinning .

He had just killed his wife.

Horrified with himself, Paul stumbled backwards and grabbed onto the edge of the kitchen counter. His mind began playing a flashback of that night Claire came upon him sitting in the backyard, wiping at tears and taking swigs of a nearby flask.

"Whoa. I smell alcohol, so I know something's wrong," Claire had exclaimed, stepping out onto the brick paver patio.

Paul had quickly wiped beneath his eyes, turning his face away.

"I lost a patient today," he had mumbled.

"Lost? What does that mean, lost?"

"One of my patients, the one I told you about. You remember, Evangeline? The hospital called and said that she suffered cardiac arrest while in labor this morning."

"Oh my God! She was young, wasn't she? That's terrible!" Claire had covered her mouth with her hand.

Paul had sighed and refilled his glass from the flask on the patio table.

"Yes, she was only...about 29. Tragic. I've never experienced this before. And I know I wasn't her GP, but I feel the same sense of sadness, hopelessness as they must feel." Paul had turned to look at Claire's face before turning away as his eyes welled up again.

"I was still her doctor – one of her doctors – and I feel like I should have helped her more."

"What more could you have done? You weren't responsible for her choices after she was released from the hospital. What about the child's father?"

Paul hesitated as he thought of a response.

"There was no record of the father. She refused to cooperate. And as a legal adult – especially once she was certified sane and able to live on her own – we had no way to force her to reveal the father."

"Gosh, that's so incredibly sad. Perhaps he'll come forward once he finds out...you know..."

"I hope so. The baby deserves that much," Paul added, taking another drink.

Claire had reached over and gently removed the flask from his hand.

"Look, this isn't the way. You know that. You'll be flat on your ass tomorrow," she had said as she began stroking his knee.

They had sat together quietly in the yard, listening to the sounds of birds chirping and the occasional shout from kids playing nearby.

"You know what?" Claire began.

The kids shouted again.

"Uh, never mind."

"What? Finish your thought?"

"I was just thinking – I know it's super crazy, and it's just an inkling of a thought, but..."

"But what?"

"I mean, you've told me that this girl had no family and

almost no past. And if the baby's father doesn't step up, well... I think you know where I'm going with this."

Claire had opened the flask and taken a sip for herself, then gagged, laughing.

"This is pretty awful!"

"Just spit it out, hon! You're stalling. Why?"

"What if... what if *we* looked into maybe seeing if, possibly, we could *adopt*...the - *her* baby?" She had spoken slowly, evenly, before taking another sip from the container. That time, she had not gagged. Claire had faced her husband with that steadfast and determined look in her eyes that he knew all too well.

"You know we've always wanted to have another baby."

Paul threw up both his hands. "You're moving way too fast on this. Let's just slow down, alright? The mother just passed this morning!"

"I know! I know! But I just want to put it out there so that when that conversation begins – you were her therapist, so you'll be privy to at least some of the information. You can kind of just see... that's all I'm saying, just *see*."

Paul knew his wife quite well after so many years together. Paul had known that she didn't want to *just see*. She was already building a plan in her mind, and sitting next to her, Paul had almost been able to hear the gears turning.

It would be nearly six years before they were able to legally start the process.

Claire had fought for that kid as if she had pushed him out of her own womb; as if he had been mistakenly caught up in red tape and she just needed to get him back home.

All the while, Paul laid awake at night wondering when he would get a call that the court wanted to get a sample of *his* blood for a DNA test. Of course, that had never happened, why would they even suspect him?

And now, it had all come down to those final moments when he'd had to defend his honor – his family's honor. In his mind, it was a small enough sacrifice to keep his secret.

Despite wanting to sit to read the pages of the journal for himself, Paul had to start cleaning up. There wasn't enough time before the boys would return home from school. And he couldn't risk Leo discovering that the journal was missing. Perhaps Paul could talk to him and compel him to hand it over, or he could suggest that they read it together. After all, Paul was a therapist! He should be able to work that into a treatment plan!

Leo's backpack lay at the bottom of the stairs, next to Claire's body. Paul went to retrieve it, his stomach churning as he noticed that Claire's eyes were still open, staring and accusing.

"I'm so sorry, babe," he said, using his foot to slide the backpack away, before opening the main compartment and dropping the book inside.

Once he got back to the top floor, Paul spent a few more minutes practicing the appropriate amount of audible grief before dialing 911 to report his wife's misfortune.

BREADCRUMBS

On the day of Claire's funeral, Craven noticed that the heavens mourned too. It was only fitting that a storm of rain, lightning and thunder crashed down from the sky – without a single ray of sunshine to bid farewell to the incredible woman who had just seen her final sunrise. It was poetic in a sense. The world didn't deserve to be blessed with a beautiful day when they were saying goodbye.

Every row of the church was filled with Claire's friends and family, as well as others who just knew her briefly, but who had still been touched by her in some way. She'd had that effect on people. They couldn't help but be drawn by Claire's warm smiles, gentle voice and kind heart. Seeing so many people pile into the church – even on such a dreary day - to send her off, gave Craven a warm feeling inside, knowing that she would be remembered so fondly.

No one ever expects to lose their parent at a young age, especially not through a household accident like falling down stairs. It didn't make any sense at all, and try as he may, Craven couldn't picture a scenario where his mom failed to grab the rail to catch her fall. Her last moments gnawed at his subconscious and he couldn't stop himself from trying to piece it all together. But there were no answers to be found as his father would only repeat that he had found her as she was.

Stoic throughout the ceremony, Craven felt close to breaking when it was time to walk past the casket one last time before the attendants closed the lid and transported his mother to her gravesite.

His father signaled for Craven and Leo to go ahead of him as they approached the casket. Leo hopped in front to climb up on the small stool and reach the opening; for the first time since they'd arrived, Craven realized Leo was wearing the backpack. He had been so lost in his grief that he didn't notice it – or smell it – on the ride over in the limo. But he could see now that Leo had the bag strapped snugly around his shoulders, and the way he so boldly stepped in front made Craven feel like the other boy was taunting him.

Craven swallowed hard and tried to push back his anger as he watched Leo place both of his hands on top of Claire's, folded just below her chest. To onlookers, it was a touching moment, a son saying a goodbye to his adoptive mother; but the sweet moment enraged Craven because, from where he stood, he could see what Leo was doing with his hands.

His fingers stroked hers, pausing to poke and pinch the loose skin on the knuckle. Then he touched her face and traced the shape of her mouth with his fingers. Craven had seen Leo play with his dead pets in the same manner, poking and pushing the skin around. He was repulsed to see him *playing* with his mom as if she were one of his carcasses.

He resisted the urge to push Leo off of the stool and away from Claire. He didn't want Leo touching his mother with his creepy hands; he shouldn't be anywhere near her. To be quite honest, if Leo hadn't been at school when the accident happened, Craven would have suspected he was somehow involved. Craven hadn't forgotten about the Taylors, and while he still had no solid proof of Leo's involvement, he had evidence. And now that his mom was no longer there to stick up for him, there was a chance Craven could work on getting Leo sent back to whatever hell he had come from.

When Paul stepped forward to stand next to his wife, he seemed to be overcome by his emotions. Craven watched as his dad grabbed the side of the coffin for balance as he shook uncontrollably, crying loudly, calling out her name. His cries reverberated through the room.

"Claire, honey, I'm so sorry," he sobbed. Next to him stood his good friend Pharaoh, who put his arm across Paul's shoulders to support him.

Pharaoh stood with Paul at the casket, holding him up and letting him express his pain until, after a few minutes, he leaned over and whispered into Paul's ear. Paul immediately straightened up and stopped crying. He placed a gentle kiss on Claire's forehead and then turned and walked down the aisle behind Pharaoh.

Pharaoh stood out in the church, as he did at every gathering. With his towering near-seven-foot frame and the stunning contrast of his dark skin against the pear-colored suit, and the ever-present newsboy cap perched atop his head - he easily commanded the attention of every room he entered. All eyes followed him as he glided down the aisle towards the foyer of the church, where he stopped with Paul and his sons.

"How are you doing, buddy?" Pharaoh tapped Craven on the arm. "If you need to talk, I'm here for you as well."

"You too, little guy," he addressed Leo. "My line is always open, day or night."

Craven opened his mouth to respond, but his words were forgotten as he watched what happened next with surprise.

Leo rushed forward and wrapped his arms around Pharaoh's legs in a tight embrace. Tears welled up in his eyes and spilled down his cheeks as the child clung to him. Pharaoh laughed nervously and reached down to give Leo a gentle rub on his shoulder.

Paul stepped forward and pried Leo off of the man, apologizing profusely.

"Oh, it's quite alright! No worries!"

Leo tried to pull away from Paul to run back to Pharaoh, but Paul pushed him away.

"Maybe you should come by soon so we can all talk," said Paul.

"Definitely, let's make it happen," Pharaoh opened the heavy wooden door and held it for Paul and his family.

"I'll be seeing you all real soon."

THE RIDE HOME in the limo was silent.

Craven took a pump from his inhaler as he angrily eyed Leo in the seat across from him. But Leo kept his eyes focused on the world passing by outside. The backpack was on the floor, between his feet, and Leo tapped his heel against it as if he were keeping time with a song in his head.

His complete disconnect with the world around him was beginning to get on Craven's last nerve. Then the freaky poking of mom in the casket. He had treated her like some kind of *thing*. And what was that big display of affection to Mr. Pharaoh all about?

Craven glared at him from across the seat, hoping he would respond and they could get into it, get it all out, right then and there with Dad as witness and mediator. They could clear the air about so many things.

"Dad, any more news about what happened to the Taylors?" asked Craven, with his eyes fixed on Leo's face.

"They're still investigating. Not much is being released to the public, but they don't have a suspect yet. They think it was related to some of their drug dealing or related to maybe the... trafficking." Paul turned in his seat to look at Craven and Leo. "You don't have to worry about anything happening to us. That was an isolated incident by some psycho."

"Some psycho is right," agreed Leo, tossing a wide grin toward Craven.

When they arrived home, Craven stormed up to his bedroom and slammed the door. He paced back and forth, and he grew angrier as he thought about how much life was going to suck from here on out. It just didn't seem fair that his mother was gone, but Leo and his dead pets were still here.

Craven's dad yelled up the stairs that he and Leo were going to get ice cream, and if Craven wanted to come along, he could. He didn't want to, but knowing they were leaving together felt like a gift.

Craven waited until he was sure they were gone before he raced downstairs and began looking around for the backpack. Leo had gotten away with taking it to the funeral, but Craven was certain that his dad wouldn't want that disgusting smelly bag on the backseat nor anywhere in the car.

It wasn't in the closet or beneath the sink. It wasn't in the mud room. Just as Craven was about to push down his nerves to check in the basement, he spotted one of the straps sticking out from behind the sofa. Sure enough, the backpack was wedged against the wall.

Craven had to work fast. He carried the bag through the house and out into the backyard where he dropped it into one of the trash cans and replaced the lid. He thought more about it, then added several bags of trash on top of the backpack for added insult, then closed the bin again.

It wasn't much, but it was something. It was a statement from him to Leo, and it gave Craven a tiny sense of satisfaction in the moment.

"Take that, weirdo," he laughed. "That's for mom."

After all, why should Leo get to keep anything that he loved, when Craven just suffered such an unimaginable loss?

PAUL THOUGHT of Pharaoh as a charismatic, skillful therapist and friend, but behind that façade were centuries of evil.

Centuries.

Pharaoh was only the latest incarnation of an ancient demon spirit meant to spread chaos and corruption. For several lifetimes, he'd slipped in and out of history, taking on different characteristics, personas and identities, including roles as high as the advisor to a King, or sometimes as simple as... well, a trusted psycho-therapist. He stepped into whichever skin he needed to get the job done.

This time, he had needed to help usher in a new young demon.

In his current earthly role as a psychiatrist, he had the special ability to sniff out the vulnerabilities of the humans he worked around, and thus begin subtly manipulating both patients and proteges like Paul Bennett. It gave Pharaoh a thrill to corrupt human souls, but patience was the key to his long game.

By selecting Paul to sire a child with his "sister" Evangeline, Pharaoh had – in a sense – planted the seeds. This unholy union would continue Pharaoh and Evangeline's cursed bloodline and had produced an heir to continue their dark legacy.

Each time Pharaoh had the chance to whisper to Evangeline, he had intentionally stoked her delusions. She was in denial about who she really was, and he couldn't be bothered to break it all down for her. Well, he'd tried a few times, but she'd just started screaming and flailing until someone showed up with a needle filled with enough drugs to knock her out again. So, Pharaoh moved ahead with some minor adjustments to the plan that had been put into place hundreds of years before.

When he bumped into Paul that first day at the hospital, he knew immediately that he was the one. Pharaoh could smell the desperation coming through Paul's pores. The man needed a friend, and Pharaoh would be the friend he needed. Dropping Evangeline into his lap, figuratively speaking, Pharaoh ensured that Paul would be weak in her presence, and that their tryst would result in conception.

Then he had simply waited for Leo to arrive, his faithful apprentice ready to be molded into a vessel of evil. Evangeline was finally able to rest after centuries of service, and one day soon, her son would make her proud.

Behind his caring façade, Pharaoh was really just watching and waiting for Leo to fully awaken in his power. Tragedy and trauma were most efficient for accelerating the growth of young demons, so when he heard about the horrific massacre of the Bennett's neighbors, Pharaoh felt a little emotional. And proud.

Might Leo's rebirth come sooner than later? That unexpected embrace after the funeral confirmed Pharaoh's suspicions. It might soon be time to reveal his true self to his buddy Paul in order to begin ushering Leo into his birthright.

Pharaoh eagerly anticipated that moment of liberation when he would unleash his full monstrous glory. Until then, he would keep playing the part of healer and confidante, secretly puppeteering humanity's destruction.

A LITTLE BIT
OF EVIL

Leo sighed as he retrieved his backpack from the garbage can and examined its contents. Everything looked in order. The journal was there in the pocket. The pets were all accounted for. He'd counted them twice.

He dumped the bag and shuffled the animals apart with his hands.

"Craven wants to play," he whispered, carefully stacking each of the corpses into a pile. It was a game that Leo and his pets had played often, usually in a quiet, secluded spot of the basement where no one else would interrupt. But now it was time to let Craven in on the action.

Moving his hands back and forth across the mound of carcasses, Leo pressed down firmly, molding them together. Their tiny frames cracked under the pressure, but he ignored the breaking of bones and continued to press until they began to mold into each other.

He stepped back and watched the transformation take

place; the merging and blending of dead cells and dried tissue until there was only one form, breathing and trembling.

It slid off the side of the table and dropped to the floor at Leo's feet, then began to stretch and grow upward until it stood eye to eye with Leo. Or, make that, eye to eye to eye, as there were now 6 sets of eyes in the creature, and it had not stopped growing.

Up, up it went, stretching towards the ceiling. The creature appeared to have recycled the most useful parts of the animals and generated something different each time Leo conjured it up. This time, it sported 6 animal snouts that jutted out of various parts of its upper body. The mouths gaped open and closed as if searching for something to satisfy their desires. Furry paws extended from where front legs should be, and Leo's creature had 6 sets of claw-tipped appendages jutting from both sides of its huge body. Each was perfectly aligned to lock an enemy inside of their grip and squeeze it while using its claws to peel away the skin.

It was the epitome of every child's most disturbing nightmare, come to life at Leo's command. But Leo wasn't afraid. He was well acquainted with this beast. It was, after all, his own creation, and it specifically did Leo's bidding.

He gently stroked the side of its neck as it shivered and snorted, anxious to begin.

"Let's go find him," Leo whispered to his *friend*.

The thing followed dutifully, six long, rodent-like tails dragging behind, knocking over everything within its path.

LEO HAD the element of surprise on his side when he caught

Craven relaxing in the living room as if he hadn't started the whole thing.

The beast had pummeled Craven a bit, then toyed with him by letting him run through the house, feeling as if he had a chance of getting away. Leo trailed behind and observed the beauty in its movements. How it used its talons to threaten and keep their prey contained before it went in for the kill.

It had ripped the Taylors to pieces after chasing them through the house for fun.

Leo mostly laughed and followed it around, watching. The Taylors had run and screamed and tried to escape, but they weren't as fast as the beast Leo had created.

CRAVEN WAS MORE terrified than he'd ever been in his life, and he knew without a doubt that if he didn't run now, Leo's furry friend was going to finish him right then and there.

Finding strength in the reality of certain death, Craven lunged up and punched at his 'brother,' striking Leo in the jaw, and causing him to fall backwards just long enough for Craven to escape the living room.

But as Craven turned to run, Leo's thing charged into the room. It pushed Leo aside so that it would have full clearance to Craven.

Instinctively, Craven kicked high and hard, his foot connecting with the soft midsection of the creature.

The hit did little to slow the monster down. Craven's brain didn't even have time to figure out exactly what it was looking at, but he knew that this thing wasn't human, and he knew that he had to get away.

The beast roared – each of its snouts opened wide and emitted high pitched squeals that together were painful to human ears.

Craven took the moment to try for another escape, slipping off his shoes and deciding that hiding behind the heavy blackout curtains was a more realistic option than making it to the front door and out of the house.

Leo snatched open the curtain and grinned, taunting Craven for a moment before stepping aside and letting the creature move in.

"LEO!"

Leo and the beast turned at the sound of Paul screaming Leo's name as he and Pharaoh walked in the front door.

Paul's eyes were wide with fear as he looked around the room, trying to make sense of the scene in front of him.

"What is going on here? What-what is that thing?" He stammered and pointed at the slobbering creature that stood next to Leo, panting and drooling from each of its multitude of snouts. He turned to look at Pharaoh for help understanding the hellish sight, but Pharaoh had begun convulsing, transforming into something inhuman, right in front of their eyes.

"Pharaoh-" Paul took a step back, in fear, as Pharaoh began to sweat and tremble. A series of incomprehensible noises roared from his throat as his face distended and contorted. His body writhed beneath his clothes, bulging under an armor that covered his back and a thin layer of fur that covered the rest of his body. Razor-tipped talons tore through his shoes as hooves burst free and leather fell to the side.

A set of horns sprouted from the top of Pharaohs head and his pupils turned black.

His transformation complete, Pharaoh stood tall again. Only this time he was something undeniably evil. His tongue, dark red, slithered in and out between a mouth of sharp, even teeth with pointed tips.

Suddenly, Leo began to moan and shake, as he too began transforming into a miniature version of Pharaoh. Smaller horns pushed their way out on either side of his head and his pupils turned completely black. Both loomed, fearful and menacing as they turned to face Paul and Craven.

Craven had ducked behind his father when Pharaoh started to change, but now they clung to each other as they watched, horrified. They didn't know if they should run or if they would be safer staying put in the face of such evil.

"Paul, my friend. I hate to break this to you, but we've got a little problem," Pharaoh quipped, rows of teeth flashing in the light. "I'm afraid I haven't been quite honest with you."

"I'm confused, what—what are you?" Paul asked, his voice shaking.

"I'm something you would never understand. I've been here for hundreds of years, along with my sister who you were so kind to care for. You remember Evangeline, don't you?"

Paul nodded, nervously. He felt bile creeping up from his stomach.

Pharaoh raised his large hand and showed sharp nails at the tips of his fingers. "Of course, you remember her. How could you forget?"

Paul looked at Leo, expecting to see some kind of sympathy or connection, but Leo appeared even less human than Pharaoh. He stood, quietly, and panted like an animal, sticking his tongue out every few seconds to feel around his new sharp fangs.

"Don't be frightened. This was destiny. There was nothing you could do to stop it. But thank you, kind sir, for playing along so graciously. Thank you for your, should I say, *service*." Pharaoh's voice dripped with both dread and mirth.

Paul's face turned grey as he remembered Claire and what he himself had done. Pharaoh read his mind – as he had been doing since they'd met. He grinned.

"There's a little bit of evil in all of us, my loyal friend. Let's be honest - without us bad guys, how will everyone else know they're good? But I must admit, you actually surprised even me! I mean, I didn't expect you to knock off sweet Claire." Pharaoh shook his head, mocking disappointment. "You're truly a man after my own dark heart. I think that's why we were such good friends, really. I knew you had it in you!"

He playfully slapped Paul's arm. "If I was going to let you live, I might have to make you one of my lieutenants."

Paul opened his mouth to protest, but Pharaoh raised a sharp claw and drew it quickly across his throat, severing the jugular and sending a geyser of blood into the air.

Paul was dead before his body hit the floor.

Pharaoh uttered a high-pitched giggle while using his hoof to poke at his buddy's corpse. "What a shame. He had so much potential, but also a little too emotional for my taste."

He turned to Leo and extended his hand.

"Time to go, my boy. We've got many miles to cover, and much havoc to wreak along the way."

"What about Craven?" Leo asked, pointing to his brother, cowering in the corner. Craven's eyes darted between the beast and Leo, before him, and his father's body in its widening pool of blood.

Pharaoh sniffed at the air, his snout wiggling as he inhaled deeply, loudly. "I think we leave him to tell the story. Who would believe him anyway?"

Craven felt his lungs begin to tighten as a mixture of dread and relief washed over him.

"I-I-I won't...say anything!" He managed to wheeze. A tear fell from his eyes.

Leo chuckled, then sauntered slowly toward Craven and bent over to meet his eyes.

"We could have had such fun together," he whispered, his words slid between his lips wrapped in a hiss that made Craven's skin crawl. "We could have been real friends."

Craven forced his eyes to look away, but every spot of the room was splattered with blood and it tore at his soul.

"Just leave me, I won't say anything," he repeated, avoiding the boy's eyes. He moved his hand slowly to feel for his inhaler, careful not to startle Leo or give the impression that he was going to fight; there was no fight left in him. He had no idea what his life was going to be like if they let him live, but he knew he didn't want to be disassembled in the manner Pharaoh had handled his father.

Leo stood up and chuckled again as he turned and walked back to Pharaoh. They nodded at each other, a silent understanding that apparently it was safe to leave Craven behind, intact.

Craven exhaled and allowed his tears to fall as he warily watched the demonic pair begin their departure.

The two exited the blood-splattered room, hand in hand. Pharaoh - a majestic, hulking creature with rippling muscles beneath thick smoke colored fur- dipped his head and shoulders to cross the doorway. Leo followed dutifully, child-like, his angelic features returned except for when he turned to cast a final glance at Craven. His eyes glowed red and he flashed that same set of fangs that, just moments earlier, he'd threatened to use to tear his flesh apart.

And Leo's pet, whatever it was, walked upright and swung extended paws at its side like arms. The snouts had retracted inside of the beast's plump body, and its massive rodent tail dragged behind, knocking over everything in its wake. A menagerie of dead pets and nightmares, it breathed on Leo's command and trotted eagerly to continue to do his bidding.

Thank goodness for the cover of the night, Craven thought, stunned and alone amidst the bloodbath. He felt pity for any poor soul that might happen upon the unholy trio as they made their way to their next stop.

THE END

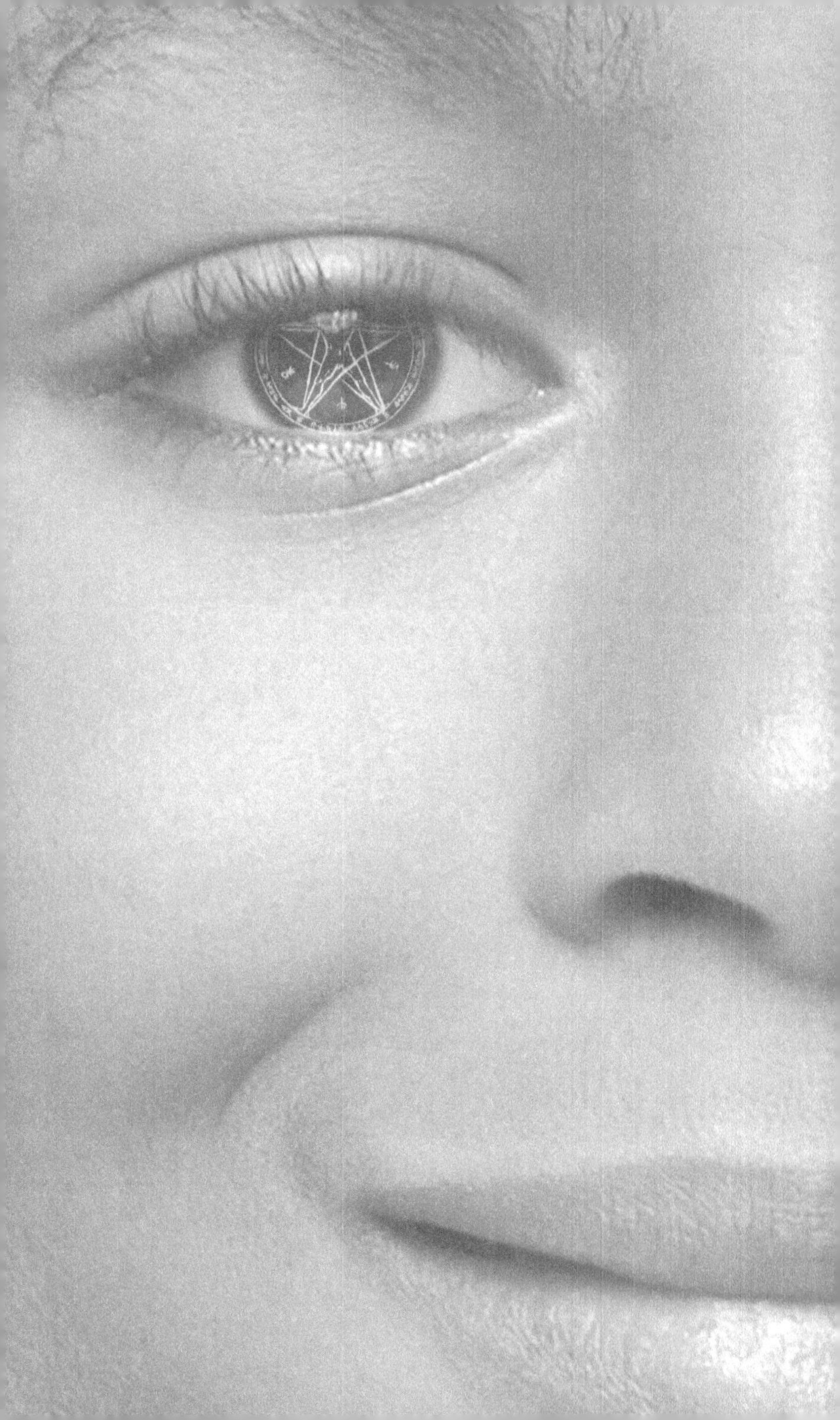

ABOUT THE AUTHOR

As a child, Kenya realized that her entertainment choices leaned more toward ghosts and goblins than princesses and fairy godmothers. She began writing short-form horror in her teens but didn't release her first book until many years later, thanks to the beauty of self-publishing. Although she may occasionally drop a work of romance *(only of the darker variety, no Romeo and Juliet over this way!)*, her real passion is weaving stories about monsters – both the kind that come from the pits of hell or may just be your neighbor.

When not staring at a blank page trying to conjure up the words, you might find Kenya shooting at the undead in her VR headset. Fun fact – Kenya collects Funko Pops of black horror movie icons.

Learn more about Kenya by visiting:
http://www.kenyamossdyme.com

We want to thank our readers for their support and enthusiasm. Your passion for stories fuels our commitment to bring you the horror that is strange and horrifying in the best of ways.

We appreciate any and all reviews, so help us out by leaving your thoughts online.

Thank you again for spending your time with us and remember to...

......EMBRACE YOUR STRANGE!

Follow us everywhere:
@trubornpress
www.trubornpress.com

PROGENY

CONTENT WARNINGS

- MENTAL HEALTH ISSUES
- VIOLENCE
- ANIMAL CRUELTY
- GORE & BODY HORROR
- DEATH & DYING
- SUPERNATURAL ELEMENTS
- CHILD ENDANGERMENT
- SEXUAL & ROMANTIC MISCONDUCT